Praise for *Slack-Tide*

'I finished *Slack-Tide* after a heady, intense few days of reading. Elanor Dymott writes with such lucidity and precision; her characters, setting and premise are real and involving – I enjoyed it immensely'

Laura Barnett, author of *The Versions of Us*

'*Slack-Tide*, Elanor Dymott's captivating third novel, is sharp in many ways... It's so convincingly – and, at times, so disastrously – funny... But what makes *Slack-Tide* distinct is its brilliant depiction of both romantic rapture and heartfelt delusion'

Daily Telegraph

'Forensic and spare, *Slack-Tide* is a persuasively messy (and sinister) tale of mixed-up emotions'

Metro

'A compelling and beautiful reflection on the stories that hold us together and keep us apart'

Sarah Moss, author of *Ghost Wall*

'Dymott writes particularly well on sex, and is refreshingly comfortable with the ambiguities at play in each encounter. This psychologically intelligent study... packs a very precise punch'

Financial Times

'Well written, amusing and, as you'd expect, intelligent...
highly readable'

Bookmunch

'*Slack-Tide* is hypnotically compelling. It asks how you can
ever get the measure of your own needs, let alone the needs
of another, and how difficult it is to mesh your life with
theirs. Her lovers are experienced, flawed, damaged and
demanding, but she won't let them be fooled or floored by
emotion... Dymott shows that what you want is not always
what you need. That the price exacted by finding yourself
can be having to let another go'

Marina Benjamin, author of *Insomnia*

'Sharp and potent, this novel explores what it's like to fall
in love and have your heart broken. We are spared any
idealised notion of romance. Instead we get passion at its
most convincing: flawed, irrational and wild'

Literary Review

'*Slack-Tide* by Elanor Dymott is about a love that arrives
unbidden in the wake of a tragedy. It is beautifully written
and had me sobbing'

Observer

ELANOR DYMOTT

Elanor Dymott was born in Chingola, Zambia, in 1973. She read English at Oxford, then practised law in London and in South East Asia before becoming a law reporter for *The Times* and the Incorporated Council of Law Reporting. She lives in London, where she is a Consultant Fellow for the Royal Literary Fund.

ALSO BY ELANOR DYMOTT

Every Contact Leaves A Trace
Silver and Salt

ELANOR DYMOTT

Slack-Tide

VINTAGE

1 3 5 7 9 10 8 6 4 2

Vintage
20 Vauxhall Bridge Road,
London SW1V 2SA

Vintage is part of the Penguin Random House group of companies
whose addresses can be found at global.penguinrandomhouse.com

Copyright © Elanor Symott 2019

First published in Vintage in 2020
First published in hardback by Jonathan Cape in 2019

penguin.co.uk/vintage

A CIP catalogue record for this book is available from the
British Library

ISBN 9781784709334

Printed and bound in Great Britain by Clays Ltd, Elcograf S.p.A.

Penguin Random House is committed to a sustainable future for
our business, our readers and our planet. This book is made from
Forest Stewardship Council® certified paper.

Contents

Prologue

Slack-Tide is the period of quiet water between flood and ebb currents, when there is no perceptible flow in either direction.
Chapman Piloting & Seamanship
(67th edition)

From Paris once, he brought me a miniature wind-up music box that played Bizet. His other present, which I'd asked for, was a leaf from the Tuileries Gardens. He slipped it in the pocket of my yellow Moleskin diary, then traced its shape with a red pen and wrote the word 'INSIDE'.

Now, if I search for a date or a memory, I am caught by the bold red leaf. Just the tip of its twin emerges, dark green and pressed flat by the year.

His business was designing cities. He'd started out with houses, though by the time we met he did that only for friends. I liked being able to call him 'my American architect', as if I'd hired him to build me a home.

In the December that we were introduced, by what he termed 'the accidental agency' of my friend Susie, I turned forty. He was fifty-two, and had been let go by his wife.

One evening I left the library early and went to his apartment.

'How much did you miss me?' I asked.

'This much.' He held his hands as if in prayer then he moved them away from each other until they were behind his head.

Making love to me later, he paused.

'These are the parts I will miss most –' he touched my underarms – 'when you decide you're through with me. Here,' he said, drawing his fingers across my skin, 'and here.'

When my broken heart was starting to mend I went for lunch with my brother.

'An architect and a novelist?' Will said. 'It was never going to work.'

'What do you mean?'

'I mean, a big part of his job is drawing plans for buildings that will never be built.'

'And?'

'And a big part of yours is dreaming up non-existent people, who you talk about as if they're real.'

'But they *are* real to me. When I write them, they *are*.'

'I rest my case,' my brother said. 'All the poor guy ever did was try out some ideas. You took him literally. You fell for everything he said.'

It's the pictures I paint that trip me up.

This time, I sketched a hinterland from the line of a stranger's back as he stood in a cafe on a winter afternoon. When he turned and held out his hand and said, 'I'm Robert. And you must be Elizabeth,' I was unprepared for what was to come. By midsummer the thing between us was finished, and it was as if a storm had torn the roof from over me.

December

At a certain minimum altitude, perhaps a few feet above the ground, we must decide if we can see enough ahead of us to make the switch from instruments to visual flight. If we cannot – if we are still in cloud, or snow or heavy rain or fog or whatever incarnation of high water might be impeding our view of the runway – then we abort the landing.

Mark Vanhoenacker, *Skyfaring: A Journey with a Pilot*

I picked up Susie's message on my way to the library.

'Can you do me a favour?' She was out of breath. 'Or can you do a friend of mine a favour? No, actually, make that a guy I know. Can you do a guy I know a favour? We were supposed to go to a movie tonight. Tom is sick, so I have to stay home. So this guy – Can't explain in a message. I need you to be my stand-in. Call me! He's lovely. You'd like him. I'm taking Tom to the doc's, but call.'

Frowning and smiling together, I phoned.

'Are you crazy?' I asked. 'Why would I go to the movies with a guy I'd never met?'

'Why not?' she said. 'I would, if I hadn't had a relationship for four years. Sorry. Sorry, Liz! I just meant –'

She told me he was an architect. Halfway through a divorce. Or a separation, one or the other. A really lovely, polite, clever guy. Came across as quite mysterious, but he always seemed kind, and nice.

'How do you know him?' I asked. 'Why are you meeting mystery guys? You're so married.'

'Book group. Showed up a few months ago. Said he wanted to meet new people. He's the only guy, it's quite sweet. He's obviously lonely. He's American. We all think he's really hot. I guess he doesn't have many friends in London, you know, for going out with.'

'So?'

'So I said I'd take him to the movies. We've never talked much. Just books, and there are always tons of people, and I thought it would be good to be friendly, make him feel welcome. And now Tom is ill.'

'Can't Ben look after him?'

'Working late.'

'So call your mystery man and cancel. It's 9 a.m. He's got all day to find someone else.'

'He hasn't. That's the whole point. He's on a flight from New York right this second. He'll get off the plane and go straight to the cinema and I'll just basically have stood him up. It was supposed to be this really nice thing and it'll just be horrible.'

'Which cinema?'

'The Soho Curzon.'

'If it was any other day I'd say yes. I'm doing two hours at the library, tops, then I'm going Christmas shopping. I can't just drop everything because of some guy from your book group.'

'Oh, Liz. All you have to do is show up, see a nice movie with a nice guy, end of story. Say yes, I'll love you forever. Even if you don't get on, it'll be good for you to meet someone new. And he's pretty gorgeous.'

'You're setting me up!'

'I am not. Well, I sort of am. Don't think of it like that. Think of it as doing me a favour.'

'What if we don't get on?

'What if you do? Look. He's interesting. And if he isn't your kind of guy, you know.'

'You know, what?

'Introductions lead to introductions. He's an architect. He'll know other architects.'

'What's so great about architects?'

'Just try it out. That's all I'm saying.'

'What's his name?'

I found Robert online. In a talk called 'Urban Utopias', he moved his hands a lot. I zoomed in. His fingers were long and slender. He spoke in a careful voice, enunciating each word. He was tall, with broad shoulders and big arms, and a shock of thick, dark hair. I imagined what it would be like to be held by him.

He wore a dark blue suit in velvet or moleskin, which hung loosely. His shirt was crisp and white, and his tie pencil-thin. He had a short beard, and his glasses hailed from another era; I'd seen ones like them only a handful of times, in American movies or style magazines.

Watching the talk again, the man I saw had a sharp mind, a past played out in university campuses, a spacious apartment done in a Nordic style, a habit of spending his leisure time in old libraries, Viennese coffee houses and European concert halls, and was capable of providing intense sexual satisfaction with just his fingertips.

If none of those things were true, I reasoned, there was always Susie's qualifier: 'Introductions lead to introductions.'

OK, I texted her. *I've never met an architect, apart from the one in* Strangers on a Train, *which doesn't really count. But don't get your hopes up. I'm going to one movie, that's all.*

In bed with Robert a month later, I drew a hand across his face.

'Was it soft?'

'What?'

'Your beard.'

'You never saw it! How d'you know?'

'Your "Urban Utopias" talk.'

'The talk? You found it online?'

'I loved it.'

'Are you serious?'

'Your beard. I loved your beard.'

'I did it for a bet. Lasted a week. My wife hated it. My son hated it.'

'And you?

He brought a book of photographs over and showed me a family scene. Everyone was seated in armchairs. He was alone in a corner, slumped low in his seat. He had his beard, and was reading a book. Lena and Philippe, sitting apart from him, watched.

Susie told me later that the movie, *Nebraska,* had been his choice. She told me too that he had asked for the six o'clock showing because he would be jet-lagged. 'Like he really had to talk me out of the nine o'clock. As if.'

She had received my text, and sent him my contact details. When he'd cleared passport control, he texted.

Would you like tea first? At 5?

Switching to email, I replied that I'd be coming from Christmas shopping so tea would be great. I was unsure I could spend an hour talking to a man I'd never met, so I said I'd prefer 5.30. I told him to call if there was a problem, and that it would be fine to reschedule. Or, if he wanted to hold out for Susie, I wouldn't mind if he cancelled altogether.

In Soho at 5.20 my phone rang.

'Now?' I said out loud when I saw his number. 'You're cancelling now?'

I was almost there so I let it go to answerphone.

'Hi, Elizabeth,' his message said. 'It's Robert. Checking in for our evening.'

I smiled: he'd joked in his email that he was grateful to Susie for finding an understudy, but that he was new to going out with women he'd never met, so I'd have to forgive him if he was shy. Listening to the rest, I smiled again, but then I frowned. 'Just letting you know I'm here, hoping you're heading this way.'

'Is that how he is?' I asked myself out loud. 'On my case before I've even arrived?'

I played the message a second time, then I pressed delete.

The front of the Curzon is floor-to-ceiling glass. He was standing at one of the tall tables, facing to the side: sharp suit, slim-fitted, a straight broad back. His thick, dark hair fell slightly over his face. I stared, wondering if he knew I was there. He shrugged his shoulders up, then down, slowly. Staring at his back, I realised I was turned on. 'Oh no,' I whispered as I opened the door. 'That wasn't the plan.'

At the table, he held out his hand and said his name, asking, 'Will you have some ginger tea?'

He passed a cup, and his hand touched mine.

'That's a lot of bags,' he said, taking them. I took them back. Is this guy for real? I wondered. Who orders tea for someone before they've arrived? Who takes a person's bags when they've just that second met?

For the next half-hour, he spoke like a chat-show host. Like a younger David Letterman or a college professor, he asked his questions rapid-fire, in a series of non sequiturs.

One of them was, 'What's your comfort food?' Before I answered, he was telling me, 'Mine's a rotisserie chicken, takeout, with a side of gratin dauphinois. My dad was French. He died when I was a kid but my mom talked about him all the time. That was his comfort food, too. She's a New Yorker, just like me. So,' he smiled, and took a breath. 'What'd you buy?'

When I'd heard his phone message, I'd thought his voice so-so. Playing it the second time I'd asked myself, could I sleep with this guy? Could I wake up to that voice? Could I listen to him speak for more than a half-hour without bailing? Now, with the lights of Shaftesbury Avenue streaking the Curzon glass, his honeyed East Coast rhythms floored me.

'What'd you buy?' he asked again, looking under the table at my bags.

'Books, mainly. Books and CDs.'

'Why?'

'That's what people asked for!'

'How do you order your books?'

The bags were clearly marked: Foyles, and Daunt Books. Susie had told me he'd lived in London eight years. He must know those are bookshops. 'Do you mean, how do I choose them?'

'No, I mean order them. How d'you order them?'

'I didn't. I went to the shop and bought them.'

He frowned as though it was me who was being slow. 'On the shelves,' he said, and 'How do you decide where to put –'

'Oh! How do I *arrange* them? By the writer's country. Or genre. Fiction, non-fiction. You know.'

'Really?' he said, as if I'd just told him I was made of moon dust. 'Seriously?'

'Seriously,' I said.

'Not alphabetically? Or by colour? Some people do it by size. I met a guy once –'

After this initial stumble there were further questions. They came quickly and grew funnier and stranger. There were so many we missed the opening credits of the movie. Weeks later, when we were lovers, he told me he hadn't really minded whether we'd watched it or not.

He'd assumed I hadn't either, and that my initial protestation at his choice of film was simply a way of playing, flirting, teasing. When he said that, I thought back to what else the Curzon had been screening that night, and reminded him that I'd pointed out two I'd rather see.

'You were going through the motions,' he said. 'Once we'd met, and started to talk, you didn't care what we watched. The movie was a pretext.'

'For what?'

'For the date. Pretty soon it was obvious we were on a date.'

'But the movie *was* the date.'

'We didn't have to see it! It was just a cover.'

'For what?'

'For this. It was a pretext for this. Come here.' He pulled me across the bed. 'Do what you did to me this morning. Slowly, though. I want to watch.'

'But –' I paused.

'But what?'

'You'd already bought the tickets. So you must've known we'd watch it.'

'Oh, honey.' He placed both hands on my upper back. 'Please. Do that thing again.'

After *Nebraska* we'd found a noodle bar on Wardour Street. We ordered, then he explained his approach to securing the affections of a woman in whom he was interested.

'She looks over her shoulder, I'm there. I put myself in her way.'

'If that doesn't work?'

'I track her. Chase her. Hunt her down.'

'And then?'

'When she's worn out, I bring her to the ground and tear her to pieces.'

He'd reached behind my neck and touched a finger lightly to my skin. 'This is where I start. This is the spot. Just here.'

I'd felt a flicker pass over my whole body, like a tongue.

He asked for the bill, then he pulled a yellow Selfridges bag from his satchel. 'I went Christmas shopping too.'

I didn't understand. He pushed it towards me, and when still I didn't, he opened the bag himself and took out a tissue-wrapped parcel which he placed in my hands. Inside was a thick, soft, black scarf, made from a kind of crinkled crêpe with deep-cut folds.

'But we've hardly even met. Why are you giving me a gift?'

'It's a nice thing to do. Susie told me you've just had an important birthday. It's nearly Christmas. I had time after my flight.'

'What if I hadn't liked it?'

'I took a chance. So, do you?'

'Yes! But why would you give me –? Oh.'

'Oh, what?'

'I've heard about guys who do that on dates! It's funny.'

'Do what?'

'They always get the woman a present.'

'I don't go on dates. I mean I haven't, not for twenty years.'

'Gosh.' I held the scarf to my face. It was soft, and thicker than it looked.

'You look good in it.'

'I haven't put it on yet.'

'You will, I mean.'

'Quite a chance to take.'

'I could have returned it, if you'd flung it back at me.'

I looked at him, and took a deep breath.

I was thirty-six when I left my husband. We'd met when I was very young, and before him, I'd had only one boyfriend, at school. A couple of years on from my divorce, I was in Clerkenwell with my French friend Magali. The trio that evening played straight-ahead jazz. By the end of the opening number she was thinking of booking them for her club, and suggested we stay for the whole set. After the break, just before they started up again, she told me she'd seen me at the bar with the bassist, and had seen him offer me a drink.

'Why did you say no?' she whispered. 'You like him, right?'

'He's cute,' I agreed.

'So why not let him buy you a drink?'

'Because I can buy my own.'

'Sheez.' She shook her head. 'What are you scared of? Promise me, next time a guy does that, see how it feels to say yes.'

'Then what?'

'Then drink it. And talk with him a bit. Saying yes to a drink doesn't mean you have to marry him. Talk for five minutes. If you don't like him, then say thank you and walk away. It's what people do. It's normal. Now let me listen to these guys. Some of us have work to do.'

At the noodle bar with Robert I looked at him holding the empty yellow Selfridges bag and I thought of Magali. 'Thank you,' I said. 'It's perfect.'

The bill came, and I picked it up.

'It's mine,' he said. I tried to point out that he'd paid for the movie, but before I'd finished my sentence he'd handed over his money.

We stepped onto the street, and he asked me if I believed in intuition.

I laughed. 'It's not a belief system, Robert.'

He struggled with my response, then he said that intuition wasn't a notion he subscribed to. 'You know how John Kennedy Jr died? Small plane, heavy weather off Martha's Vineyard? You're familiar with the story, right?'

I shook my head and he told me how, low in a storm, the president's son had seen a line of lights far off and, mistaking them for a landing strip, had ignored the plane's instrument panel and dipped the nose for landing, heading straight for the queue of little boats in the water far below. The radar track later showed evidence of the young man's vertigo as he'd gone into his death-spiral.

'It's like carsickness,' Robert said. 'It happens when you see or feel things that don't tally with what your instruments are telling you. So your brain goes into overdrive trying to reconcile it, and you're dizzy. You know what the real skill of instrument flying is, when that happens? To ignore your instincts and pull back. To listen to your mind, not your heart.'

In the British Library there is an artwork by Patrick Hughes called *Paradoxymoron*. Approaching it from one side, a passer-by will register a series of bookcases, protruding from the canvas. Each of them is positioned on the diagonal. As the passer-by continues walking, looking always at the picture, they will notice that the shelves appear to rotate. Repeating this a second and a third time, staring at this static sculpted painting, the passer-by might experience a little of the nausea Robert had spoken of.

I invited him to an event at the library.

'Keep your eyes on the picture,' I said, taking his hand and walking him past it.

'That's it,' he said. 'That's literally what I was talking about.'

Outside the noodle bar on Wardour Street he suggested sharing a cab.

I laughed. 'But you live near Angel.' Reminding him that I lived in Kentish Town, a fact he'd been careful to ascertain over dinner, I gestured that way.

'It's fine,' he said. 'We'll do a round trip.'

'You go ahead. I'll take the Tube.'

I hailed him a taxi but he waved the driver on. Trying to lift my bag from my shoulder he said, 'I'm fine with the Tube.'

'But you need a different branch.' I retrieved my bag. 'It's OK,' I said. 'We can walk to the station together, but I'm carrying this.'

While we walked, he told me that he was due to have Christmas on his own in New York; he'd see one or two old friends, but otherwise be alone. Then he'd fly to Mexico to join Lena and Philippe and their extended families. The group had rented several houses in a small town, and would spend New Year together.

I said that it was good he was able to do it, despite the separation, and that his son must be glad.

'You know what?' he said. 'I literally feel like smashing the whole thing to pieces.' Holding his hand high, he brought it down sharply like a hatchet on a log. 'Get rid of it. Be free. I don't want to go any more.'

'You'll be fine,' I said, surprised by his anger. 'You'll be glad you went.'

My ex-husband and I spent our first separated Christmas together. Just the two of us, in a house on a part of the Suffolk coast we'd always visited. On Christmas Day, we picnicked on the beach: cold lobster, hot potatoes in tinfoil, and champagne in glasses we'd brought from the house.

I took Robert there once, in the May that I was with him, but it felt like an incursion. Looking at a map of England in the library this week I was struck by how few stretches of the English coastline were free of old memories, and available for the making of new ones.

My ex-husband and I were happy that Christmas, in a strange, sad kind of a way. Thinking about it after my date with Robert, I realised that we'd been able to be happy only because things hadn't yet been decided. That we might have stayed together still. That losing our child had nearly broken us in two, but that beyond that, we weren't sure why we were pulling apart. We walked that shoreline every day, with the waves coming in from the east. Frozen in that moment, it was as though time had been suspended, and our decision postponed.

Within a year our split was official. I spent the following Christmas in London with Susie and her family. My brother and his wife had invited me to Norfolk. Their second son was newborn, though. It hurt to even think of it, so I stayed away, and promised myself to them another year. Susie and Ben had made it clear I was more than welcome. For the whole of the week I was there, though, I was a torso cut from ice.

That night with Robert, to be friendly, I went the long way round: we took the Tube together to King's Cross, where we would take our separate lines. In the final moments, he outlined his options for return flights in the New Year, and asked if I'd like to meet again.

'Yes,' I said, smiling. I put out my hand to shake his. 'Yes, I'd like that.'

Then he kissed me.

Because the act was unilateral and full on the mouth, I was puzzled and stepped back. Until then, aside from my private acknowledgement of desire, our meeting had seemed open to any interpretation: either we were at the start of what would be an engaging friendship or, in some uncharted way, we were navigating the very early stages of what might become a romance.

What he'd done by kissing me had changed things.

At my flat, I texted Magali. *Why did he have to do that?*

She phoned. 'His dad was French, you said. That is a typical French thing. A certain kind of a Frenchman would do that. Did you like him? Could you do him?'

When I told her about the scarf, she said that was a French thing too. 'Oh, that is normal. A small thing, a gift. Olivier was the same with me, some flowers, some perfume, all the time at the beginning. It's romantic, yes?'

'It's not a small thing. It's a massive thing.'

'The scarf?'

'Yes, it's thick and warm and black and crêpe-y and kind of –'

'If you don't want it I'll have it. The heating's gone again at the club. I'm permanently shivering, my musicians are shivering. They are playing in fingerless gloves. We are all completely freezing our balls.'

'I enjoyed our conversation,' I told her when we met the next day. 'My mind liked it. A part of me that's died was reminded of being alive. But he's not someone I want a relationship with.'

'Why not?' she asked.

'He's old. He's still married.'

'Separated, you said.'

'Not divorced, though.'

'Your divorce took a while.'

'He hasn't even started his.'

'Didn't you say you wanted a relationship? Isn't it time to try?'

'He's fifty-two. I don't want a man with fifty-two-year-old legs. Can you imagine? Can you even imagine?'

When there was no response, I conceded, 'I could've taken more of the conversation.'

Because Robert had insisted on paying for our dinner as well as our movie tickets, I wrote a thank-you note. He'd given me his address, and when I cycled into town the next day I took it with the pile of Christmas cards I was dropping through friends' doors. At his apartment, a converted Victorian printworks near Angel, the high metal gates were locked. I cycled on and called him to check where his office was on Fleet Street; my final destination was near there, so it wouldn't be a detour.

He answered at the first ring. 'I just left work,' he said, so loudly I held the phone away. 'Where are you? Really? That's incredible! I'm heading home. I'm walking right toward you.'

We met a second later in the street. Instead of his sharp-fitted suit, he wore chinos that were the colour of mud, and baggy. They were cut a little too short so his red socks were clearly visible. He had on an old man's winter coat and a felt hat. I was in my hi-viz cycling jacket and a red helmet. Giving each other the once-over, we grinned like teenagers, then I handed him the envelope.

In the email exchange that followed, he wrote how delighted he'd been to see me appear from the gloom, and he thanked me for my 'beautiful' note. He knew I was busy up to Christmas, but wanted to know if I would see him one more time before he went away on Friday. I replied that I had an appointment in town on Thursday morning, and could meet for coffee. His next email attached a reservation: breakfast at the Delaunay, on the corner of Kingsway and Aldwych.

'8.30,' he'd written. '*I'll be waiting for you.*'

He was at a table facing the door.

I said hello quickly, explaining that my chain had come off, so I was going straight to wash the grease from my hands.

Before I came back, I texted Susie.

Date # 2 with your American! Breakfast at Delaunay's ... Are you ready for Xmas? Is Tom counting the days? How's work? Are you still on that case?

She texted back: *I still can't believe you guys are seeing each other! Do you really like him? I'm on my way to court now, going right past you in ten.*

Ha! I joked. *Stop for a coffee.*

OK. Fab idea.

'Please,' I breathed on the way back to Robert. 'Please tell me you were joking too.'

At the table, Robert said I could eat what I liked.

'I know,' I said. 'I'm a grown-up.' He frowned, and I smiled and said, 'You paid last time. It's my turn.'

Robert cut in: he wanted something clear from the start. It was his invitation, so he'd be picking up the bill. He didn't want to argue it, so please would I promise not to? 'Think of it as a Christmas present!' he said. 'What'll you have? I've ordered oatmeal.'

I was preoccupied by the idea that Susie might appear at any moment, so I only half heard him. When my *pain au chocolat* came I cut it in two, lengthways. He watched me tease the strip of chocolate out of the first piece and eat it, keeping the empty pastry in my hand. He reached over and took the other piece from my plate. He ate it in two mouthfuls and began to tell me a story.

As a boy, he said, he'd attended a French school in New York. In his teens, and at his mother's behest, he had spent part of every summer in Paris as the guest of his great-aunt who, on account of her migraines, spent much of her time in bed with the curtains closed. When I asked him what he'd done every day, a teenage boy alone in the city, he shrugged and said he'd walked by the river, gone to the parks, and looked at art.

'Weren't you lonely?' I said.

'No. Not at all.'

If he was bored he saw an afternoon movie, or took his sketch pad to a bridge, and drew the passers-by. Early one morning, on a whim, he'd visited a patisserie. He'd chosen a *pain au chocolat* for his great-aunt, and she'd liked it so much that he'd begun to bring her one every day.

'She did what you did. Literally every single time, she tore it in two and nibbled the chocolate out, super slow! I sat there for what literally felt like forever and watched her split the damn thing right down the middle,' he laughed. Then Susie was behind me, placing her hands over my eyes and saying, 'Surprise!'

Robert stood to say hello, then they laughed about seeing one another without a novel in their hands. Robert cracked a joke about someone else in their book group, and what might be said about the two of them meeting 'in secret'. As Susie pulled up a chair and ordered coffee, I put the piece of pastry I'd been holding into my mouth and hiccupped, swallowing it whole.

Robert's oatmeal came. He took a mouthful, declared it too hot, and asked Susie about her family. She talked without stopping, so I was able to drink two glasses of water straight down, dislodging the pastry from my throat. When I tuned back in, Robert, who by now was eating his porridge, had just discovered that Susie's son was six years old.

'I can't believe I didn't know that!' He turned to me. 'It's a very studious book group. We only ever discuss literature.' Then he was plying her with anecdotes about his own son, Philippe, at that age, when he glanced at his porridge and interrupted himself to say to Susie, 'Tell me the story of when you first made oatmeal.'

Almost before she'd finished answering, he leaned in, conspiratorially.

'You wanna know mine? Well, here you go.' He shrugged his shoulders up, then down, in the way I would come to know as his habit, then he sighed. 'I was in the kitchen in our place in New York, warming Philippe's milk. We were still feeding him through the night, so it was 3 a.m. or something crazy. I took the oatmeal packet out the cupboard just for something to read. It sounded so easy I went ahead and made some. Kept me full all day. Never looked back.'

'Your wife didn't breastfeed?' Susie said.

'She extracted.' He ran his fingers through his hair.

'Ah,' Susie said. 'I totally get that. I just knew, after Tom, I couldn't have another. I didn't want my body taken to pieces again.'

'Lena was kinda shell-shocked too! We met in the summer, married in the fall and I got her pregnant on honeymoon.' He grinned.

'Wow,' Susie said, kicking me under the table.

'One morning, I looked in the refrigerator and saw these packs of extracted milk in a line,' Robert said. He stood up, suddenly, knocking the coffee cups together. 'I said out loud, "I own this fridge. I own this milk."' Then he raised his voice and beat his fists on his chest, so people turned to see. '"This is the milk of my wife which I will give to my son," I said. "I am a man!"'

Susie looked at her watch. I noticed she'd gone red. 'Oh, gosh,' she said, smiling so only I could see. 'I totally have to go. Sorry. Late for court,' and she ran, after being kissed on both cheeks by Robert, who, once he'd realised she meant what she said, had bowed at her, holding his hands together.

When Susie and Ben had brought the newborn Tom home, I stayed with them all that day and some of the next; Ben had to work, and she was exhausted. Before she got into bed, we placed the baby on a small sheepskin rug. Six hours later, when the sun had set and Susie still hadn't stirred, I stood to close the blind and became aware for the first time that this tiny boy had, in incremental wriggles and sighs, travelled more than a foot across the rug.

A year later, when I found out I was losing my own child, Susie came straight away. She held my hand, and told me I would be all right.

As Tom grew, I imagined my Phoebe alongside him, always a little younger, always invisible.

She phoned that evening, after Delaunay's.

'So he's interested in kids?'

'I guess,' I said. 'I mean, maybe. Why else would he tell that story about the milk? What do you think?'

'I think he's lovely. He's so different outside book group, but he's lovely. Nice hair. I think you should give it a go.'

'Having his kids?'

'No! Not yet, anyway. Dating him. See what happens. Oh, by the way, apart from the fact he's older, don't you think he looks exactly like Keanu Reeves?'

Robert had paid the bill for breakfast. Then he'd stood up and placed a scarf around his neck. An orange and deep-green wool, it was woven in an ornate pattern, and was more like an evening scarf than one someone would wear in the daytime. He said he'd walk me to wherever my bike was locked up, so we could say goodbye there. I explained that I wanted to walk to my appointment; there would be Christmas shoppers everywhere, I said, so it would be easier.

'May I go with you?' Robert said, putting on his hat, with its broad brim. 'I could do with a stroll.'

'Of course,' I said, smiling.

Crossing Covent Garden we kept our distance. In Soho, we meandered and he showed me buildings: the way this one leaned, how that one was clad in non-reflective glass. A light rain had begun. He described the pitch of a roof and I looked up. His voice wavered and I could hear his tongue catch, in the way mine does when I'm nervous. When I went on he hung back, then he followed.

Though I'd seen it coming, I was surprised when he paused on Argyll Street and whispered, 'Come here,' pulling me into him so I was under the brim of his hat. 'Come out the rain.'

As we kissed, our mouths opened and our tongues touched softly and I felt like I had one winter evening when, walking on my own through a nearly empty city, I'd heard a blackbird sing.

I took a train to Norfolk that afternoon. There were storm warnings, and the train's speed was restricted. My journey was five hours, rather than three. Outside Cambridge, we stopped altogether and a young man led the carriage in Christmas carols. People laughed, and strangers spoke to each other. Eventually, a couple stood up to announce their engagement, which they said had taken place as the train had pulled out of Liverpool Street. Everyone clapped and someone cheered, and hot drinks were passed around.

At the station, my brother and his children were waiting. We drove in the dark to the house, where his wife was just inside the door, with hot tea. I put my Christmas gifts by the tree, then I found Robert's text. He wished he'd given me his orange-green scarf, he said. He'd noticed that I wasn't wearing mine. There was the rain, and my journey to Norfolk would be cold, and when I arrived, the temperature would be much lower than in London. He was bothered by the fact I would quite possibly have been cold for the rest of the day, when he could've seen to it that it was otherwise.

How? I replied.

I could've given you my scarf!

You already gave me one! Anyway, you need yours, you're travelling too. Have you packed yet? Won't there be blizzards where you're headed? Won't Central Park be buried in snow?

Still, he insisted, *I should've.*

He told me later, when we'd been together a while, that it was one of the ways he'd cared for Lena, and one of the things he missed: he always made sure the boiler was in good condition, so that she was warm in the house. As well, he saw to it that the car was serviced and full of petrol, in case she wanted to go someplace. I asked him if he missed her and he thought about it, then he said, 'No. Not who she is now. But I miss who she was. I miss who we were together.'

He'd had a weekend cabin in Connecticut when they were first married. Just a tiny place, far from anywhere. It was those Connecticut weekends he thought of most. The drive there, the two of them up front, and Philippe fast asleep in the back. They talked from the minute they pulled away from Manhattan to the minute they arrived, about anything and everything, their words tumbling. In the morning, he would go out to collect wood and walk back through the snow and sometimes he would catch Lena at the window with Philippe and the light would shine out into the dark and he would run in with the logs and take Philippe and lay him by the fire and Lena would bring his coffee and they would talk all day, and Philippe would play.

He told me those stories more than once. Sometimes while he spoke, I heard the snow crunch under his feet. I sensed the cold on my own cheeks, and the warmth as he ran into the cabin. I felt the weight of the baby Philippe in my arms as he bent and lifted him, and as he placed his cheek against his son's cheek, I could smell the soft, clean skin.

By the time we met, Robert's cabin was abandoned.

Now, when he thought of it, he heard the ghosts of their voices, and saw Philippe at the head of the stairs before he could quite walk, asking to be carried down. Robert had left things in that cabin in Connecticut, and he would go back some day to reclaim them. And when the time came, he would be buried there.

That Christmas in Norfolk, there were hard frosts and starry nights. I ran across the fields and slept deeply. In the mornings, my brother and I brought in logs and heaped up the fires, and on Christmas Eve, the whole family walked to a 600-year-old chapel with paintings on its walls like frescoes. There were carols by candlelight, and spiced wine afterwards.

At sunset once, when the sky was fiery, I ran further than I ever had and saw a line of trees like fish bones against the orange sky. Robert's email that came while I was out said he'd found an article of mine online, about music which had fed into a novel I'd written, and about how each of the pieces made me feel. He was, he said, binge-listening to a song I'd matched to the sensations brought on by being kissed for the first time by 'someone I'm in love with'.

Lying in bed, I listened to the piece on my iPod. I fell asleep wondering who he was with in New York, and how he was spending his first Christmas alone.

By 27 December I was in London again. I was due to see in the New Year at Magali's club, with her and her husband, Olivier; in the days in between, I would work on the book I was trying to finish.

By then, Robert had moved on to Mexico.

He emailed that he was staying in a sprawling colonial guest house near the centre of town. It was cold, but clear after days of rain. He was woken at six by the cathedral bells, and the day was marked by those intermittent peals of sound. He wrote of paintings with oozing bloody hearts framed by golden rays, and skeletons for angels.

Philippe seemed content enough to be there. He had started at Harvard in the autumn. It was the first time Robert had seen him since he'd gone, and he was a grown-up, suddenly. Taking his son one day to a market, Robert had been pleased to notice how carefully he'd chosen the gifts he was purchasing with the money he'd been given. He wrote too about Lena: how it felt to be in the same small town as her. He was making an effort to join in ex-married events: a drinks party at his sister Charlotte's place, a few walkabouts with her husband, who was a Hollywood producer.

He'd had an opportunity to reflect on his separation, and had realised that while he could've fought harder to break through to Lena, he was thankful that he didn't have to fight any more. He was happy to be there, he concluded. He was calmer, and more hopeful about peace apart.

Every night before I slept, I read those emails again. I imagined I was there in his sprawling colonial guest house. I imagined our big iron bedstead, and soft linen sheets twisted around us when we were woken by those cathedral bells. In my imaginings, though, it was just the two of us, and Lena had never so much as existed.

Unsure how to respond to what he'd said about their split, I waited until New Year's Eve.

'It's difficult,' I wrote, 'having met you so recently and hardly knowing you, to say anything, or to know what to say, but I guess I can say well done for sticking with this plan. I am glad you are feeling calmer and more hopeful. And I feel for you, with it.'

In answer he described matadors walking down the main street, behind trumpeted and drummed fanfare. Church bells across town were calling people for the evening masses, he said. Later, he would go to a dinner his sister was hosting, and on to Jardin for fireworks and dancing. Then there was a postscript which made my heart jump.

And I like writing to you even though we barely know each other. Like crossing a river by feeling the smooth stones in the riverbed.

I was late for Magali and Olivier, and replied quickly.

I'm glad you like writing to me. I like the way you write and the spaces you leave.

In between things today, I've wondered: are we crossing your river together or did we start from opposite banks, to try to meet in the middle? Are we wading, or swimming?

At the club, I was happy. I knew that Robert would have received my email and would be thinking about me. I texted Susie to say Happy New Year and added, *I'm not sure, but I think I might just be falling for your American.*

Just before midnight, I texted Robert in Mexico. When he replied straight away, I knew that something had begun.

Six months on, when it was all over between us, a friend invited me to the end-of-year summer show at the Cass School of Art and Architecture in east London. Waiting at the gate, those glasses Robert had worn in his 'Urban Utopias' talk, that I'd thought of as unique to him, were everywhere, so that the scene was like that Kruger photograph of eyeballs strung on wires. By the time my friend arrived, I had counted fifty pairs.

January

*In both normal boat-operation and racing, certain stand-on vessels
have priority in crossing or overtaking situations, or at turns in
races; the other give-way vessel must yield … the boat on star-
board-tack … will have the right-of-way under most conditions.*
Chapman Piloting & Seamanship (67th edition), Appendix F

Robert emailed that he was due back to New York on the
morning of the 2nd. There were warnings about a storm
called Hercules, and as it turned out, his second leg from
Dallas to New York was cancelled.

*In truth, I don't really mind. I'm only slightly embarrassed to
admit to you that I've checked into the airport hotel, specifically
requesting a runway-facing room. And now at night, from my
windows, the taxiway lights are blue and green and the airliners
are hushed, climbing. It's all planning, yearning, and loveless
clarity. I feel paused.*

I replied that it was a good thing, for him to be paused between there and here. What I meant, but didn't say, was that it was good for him to have a separation between being with Lena and being with me. To have a night, at least, in a place where he was nothing to anyone.

We met for *American Hustle* at the Curzon (movie and venue, my choice), and went to a French place for dinner afterwards (his).

I was running early, not having been able to find what I wanted at the library. Approaching the Curzon I saw him striding towards me. He had one hand in his jacket pocket and was chewing gum, intently. He didn't see me until I stopped right in front of him, and reached out to touch him.

Later, he said he'd arrived early on purpose to choose the restaurant ahead of time and make sure he knew the route from the cinema. He said as well that he'd wished he hadn't been chewing gum, and had been able to kiss me properly. Instead, he'd grasped my shoulders and put his face lightly to mine and away again, his scent grandfatherly and sanitised.

He went to do his recce and we met again a half-hour later, at the cinema. I ordered a beer but he shook his head and said, 'Are you seriously having a drink before the movie? I have never seen anyone do that before.'

'I seriously am. But I'm taking it in with me, so technically, no.'

We found our seats. I got my glasses out. He wanted to try them on but I hesitated; his head was twice the width of mine. He took them anyway, holding them up so they caught the light.

'Dirty,' he said, and I flinched. He reached in his pocket for a glasses-wipe. He was a long time cleaning the lenses then he put them on. When the movie trailers had finished, I took them from his face.

The film began and he held my hand. Shrugging his shoulders up, then down, then up and down again, he sighed. After what seemed a reasonable interval, I withdrew my hand and moved slightly away.

In Anna Funder's *Stasiland*, two people who are very much in love are forcibly separated for a long time. Later, when they are reunited and living together, one of them takes a trip away. The day she returns, they meet by chance on the stairs and greet each other with just a nod, before continuing on their separate ways and going about the business of their days.

On my marriage ending, it was some time before my sadness began to lose its hold. When it did, and I could sense what it might be like to be free, the notion of such an independent togetherness became an elixir.

It was two years before I felt able to say yes to an actual date. The first was with an artist I had met at a literary festival, who had flirted over lunch and asked for my number. Walking to meet him for a concert in Victoria Park, I couldn't get beyond the feeling that I was being unfaithful to my ex-husband. When the artist kissed me at the end of the evening, I kissed him back. But when he suggested coming home with me, I said goodnight and walked away.

That summer I fell for a gardener in New York. He had grown mint in his garden and looped it with string so that it formed a lush green tube, raised above the ground, which ran around the perimeter. His garden table was built from a single plank of wood, its sun canopy fashioned from a boat's sail. Sitting at that table one night as the sky darkened, with fireflies all around us, he asked me to give up my flight to London and to stay with him. I was afraid of what that might mean, and left for the airport without saying goodbye.

In the autumn a film producer I met in Berlin invited me to travel around the world with him. I returned to London and we discussed a plan by email, but I bailed again and missed the flight I was booked on.

From that point on, I was clear with the men I met:

I didn't want to make plans ahead of time. I didn't want to hold hands in the street. I didn't want a relationship.

Magali continued to educate me in the art of being single. Most of the men I met at her club were young, and many of them musicians. In the main, they were happy to restrict their conversation to the frustrations and small victories of their own lives. Beyond wanting my opinion on their plans for their futures, they asked very little of me.

The only man who had any real difficulty with my terms was a Colombian engineer, who had decided he was ready to settle down. If I liked sex with him, he said, and enjoyed talking with him, and dancing with him, and if I wasn't against the idea of seeing him again, didn't that constitute a relationship? Couldn't he say he was my boyfriend? A fortnight later he asked me to marry him, and we went our separate ways. I'd wanted things to end less abruptly than they did, but when it came to it I was unable to express how confused I was by the idea of forever. I attempted to explain that because I'd lost my child, my husband, and everything we'd made together, I was unable to feel anything for anyone, but what came out was the baldest of statements that I felt nothing whatsoever for this man who had stood there and asked me to spend the rest of my life with him.

The summer before I met Robert, I'd stayed with some Portuguese friends, who were translators, in their weekend apartment at Tavira. They came down from Lisbon occasionally, for a few days at a time, but otherwise I was alone. Away from the distractions of London, I was able to reflect on what had happened with the environmentalist, and to see the patterns into which I'd settled.

Daytimes were hot. I swam in the early morning and walked to the end of the thin strip of sand and back until I was dry. I stayed inside the rest of the day and worked, my papers lifting and falling with the ceiling fans, then in the evenings I took my supper to the roof terrace and watched the sky turn. First it was purple, then ink-blue, then black and coated with a thick mist of stars. In the last hour of twilight, the swallows wheeled like crazy, playing and chasing.

On one of those mornings on the thin strip of sand I saw my neighbour from the apartment below, with her daughter, who was four years old. We stopped to speak and the child, Anya, asked me to help her say my name, which she couldn't pronounce.

They were there every day then, and sometimes earlier, so they joined me in the water. A couple of times, they came up for supper on my roof terrace, or asked me in to their apartment to share theirs.

One morning on the beach, my neighbour asked me to watch Anya; she had to go back for a delivery, and Anya didn't want to come. She would only be an hour, she said. I was surprised, but said yes. We sat very quietly, the little girl and I, watching the waves. Then Anya mimed, to explain her Portuguese: she would like to go for a walk, and could she please hold my hand like she did with her *mãe*?

It became our custom, Anya's and mine, to take a morning walk hand in hand while her *mãe* went back to her apartment: to clean, or cook, or to take a detour and run some errands. The little girl and I traded words and sign language. Once, we spoke for a whole half-hour in English, so that anyone passing might have thought Anya was my own daughter, and the two of us were on holiday. A ritual grew up, when Anya would sit on the end of the last boardwalk before the path back to town, and I would kneel in front of her.

'Please would you get off the dust in my feet?' she would say, and I would correct her, '"Sand", we call it. You try to say it. "Please can you dust the sand off my feet, Elizabeth?"'

'Lishbesh,' she would say, and I would take each of her tiny feet in turn and smooth the sand from her skin, gently, and stroke it from between her toes. Then I would look for her sandals in my bag and buckle them on, and we would walk home, the two of us. Sometimes, just at the last minute when the sand was all gone, I held her feet and they were warm from the sun and the sand, and made my hands warm, and we were completely still, and there was the sound of the waves.

Towards the end of my stay at Tavira my neighbour came to say goodbye; they were driving back to Lisbon for the autumn, she said, and little Anya had helped her *mãe* to make me a gift. It was an almond tart, and we went up to the roof terrace and shared it, the three of us, with some tea. Then I held the child, and she took my hair in both her hands and stroked my face with it. I laughed and she laughed. She kissed me on both cheeks and told me that she wanted to stay with me, so we could walk on the sand every single day. Her mother tickled her under her arms, and I laughed, and Anya was cross with us both until I said I'd come back next summer, and we could walk on the beach together, and everything would be exactly as it had been this time, except she might be a little taller, and I might have learned some more Portuguese, almost enough to have a whole conversation.

After they'd gone, I stayed on the terrace and watched the swallows. I felt a pain in my chest and across my back, which had come suddenly. I pulled the cushions onto the tiled floor and lay on them, looking up. The sky was in smoke-blue stripes. There was a breeze that moved the lantern back and forth. I listened to the sounds it made, until the sky was dark purple and the pain in my chest had gone, then I went in to pack.

Closing my suitcase later, I resolved that I would try for something more lasting when I got home. By putting myself in a situation where it was expected of me, I reasoned, I might learn my way back to loving: if I let someone fall for me, my logic went, I might also be able to fall for them.

It was the beginning of October when I got home. There was a party a few days later, where I drank too much and began what turned out to be an inconsequential liaison with an editor at a London literary magazine. In bed that night, he told me how many Twitter followers he had (two thousand), what it had been like to row for his university (intense), how he preferred his coffee (takeaway), and when his birthday was (that coming weekend). Ahead of the weekend I sent a birthday card to his place of work.

The last time I saw him was for *Blue Jasmine* at the Screen on the Green (movie and cinema, my choice). Going from the cocktail bar (his choice) to the cinema, he tried to hold my hand. The film was sold out apart from single seats.

I really wanted to see the movie, I said, so it didn't matter who I sat next to. Then I suggested we might as well go ahead and sit separately, since we were there and it had had good notices and wouldn't be on much longer. 'It's Cate

Blanchett!' I said when he objected. 'And Louis CK!' When he wasn't persuaded I tried another tack. 'We can go for another cocktail later, compare notes. I'll see you here, right after,' I said, pointing at the foyer carpet.

He took his place a few rows in front of me but when the lights went down he rushed past me up the aisle. Reappearing at my side a few seconds later he tugged at my sleeve. He'd found a pair of house seats at the back, he whispered.

'So?'

'So I checked with the door guy. They're not gonna use them.'

'So?'

'So, come on.'

'Oh!' I said, surprised. 'OK,' and I followed him. When the film began and he shuffled in close, though, I leaned the other way.

At my apartment later, he couldn't undo my bra. I helped him, then he lay on top of me and came before he was inside me. After that, we didn't meet again.

Sitting next to Robert for *Nebraska*, then, felt like a novelty. Doing it again the next time we met, for *American Hustle*, was a breakthrough. Reflecting on the date, I focused on that, rather than on his criticism of the state of my glasses, or the way he'd tried them on without asking, or on how, when Bradley Cooper had started going down on Amy Adams in glorious technicolour, Robert had placed two fingers to my wrist.

'What are you doing?' I'd whispered. The camera panned up and over Adams's naked body until it reached her face. As she threw back her head and began to orgasm, Robert had pressed his fingers more firmly still and held them there, whispering, 'I'm taking your pulse.'

The restaurant he had chosen was on Greek Street.

I pretended not to notice the waiter ignoring his attempts to order in French. When he'd finished, I was about to ask what he'd chosen for us but he reached into his satchel.

'It's nothing,' he said, shaking his head and handing me a slender rectangular package.

I unwrapped what appeared to be two pieces of wood, laid side by side. Looking more closely I saw brass hinges dulled by age. A series of elegant numbers was etched on the wood in black copperplate.

'I collect antique tools,' he said, staring intently at his gift. 'I saw this in an online auction, and thought of you.' He looked at me and said carefully, 'You are very measured.' Unable to help myself, I grinned. 'I'm serious,' he went on. 'You think about every single thing you say, you consider every single thing you do, I've never met anyone like you!'

Prising apart the limbs of boxwood and brass I felt my cheeks flush: at its full extent the ruler was two feet long. 'Thank you,' I said, not knowing what else to say, then I folded it back up, wrapping it in its tissue.

While we ate, Robert told me his family history, which involved an Iraqi-French opium trader, an Italian operatic tenor, a Dutch merchant and a geisha. I was able to follow quite well, until he reached the part where a young French businessman asked the American ambassador and his wife for their daughter's hand in marriage, only to be asked why on earth he would want someone so young and so foolish. From then on things became opaque. Because Robert seemed keen for me to understand every nuance, I took my notebook and tried to do a family tree while I listened. Robert pulled out a sketch pad and drew his own, with lines that were more angular than mine, and dots in a row. When I questioned the dots, he made them larger and added stick bodies and stick legs, with triangular skirts for the women and girls. He gave his sister, Charlotte, a longer skirt than all the others. 'She's very fashion-conscious.' Then he sat back and handed me the finished article.

'Finding someone to be with,' he said, holding his pen between two elegant fingertips, 'is terribly hard. You gotta draw a Venn diagram.' He turned a fresh page and drew circles, each of them overlapping. 'You gotta find the person in your diagram whose circles interlock with all of yours. What are the chances?'

'What is it with you and presents?' I sidestepped. 'Is this going to happen every time we meet?'

'You don't like it?'

'I *do*.'

Outside the restaurant, we stood on the steps. He wrapped his arms around me and held me into him. We kissed so intently that, eventually, a waiter came and tapped Robert on the shoulder. Other guests were waiting to leave, he said, and wanted to pass.

On the pavement, we kissed some more and he pulled me in closer and I could feel his erection.

'Boy,' he said. 'This is the first time I've ever kissed anyone in public.'

'Really?'

'Like this, I mean. Oh, please –'

'Please what?'

'Please will you come home with me tonight?'

'Oh,' I said. 'I can't.' He looked at me as though I was insane. 'I've got an early start. I hardly know you, and I –'

'Look, honey.' He pulled away and laughed. 'I like how measured you are. I wanted to applaud it, with my gift. But isn't this taking it a little far? It's the twenty-first century, and we've both been around the block, haven't we, more than once?'

He was frowning like a boy, so I decided against explaining that, of course, I wanted him physically, and of course I was as turned on as him, but that by not going home with him, I'd be reaching a milestone, and that if, on the other hand, I said yes, I'd likely never see him again. That for a long time now, since losing my child, all I'd been capable of by way of intimacy was sex with men I barely knew. That it had become a habit I was trying to break. That if we took it slowly, I might be able to do it more than once, and might even want to hold his hand when we walked down the street, which would be a first with any man since my ex-husband, whose hand I'd held a hundred thousand times so that it had become, through the years, an extension of my own.

'Maybe we can meet at the weekend,' I said, then I kissed him again until he agreed to let me go.

Saying goodbye, he made me promise to see him for tea at Tate Modern that Saturday. 'And dinner at my place?' he added.

'I can't promise you that. I can promise you tea, and we'll take it from there.'

I emailed Susie when I got home: I was annoyed with myself for suddenly being frightened.

'*What do you mean?*' she emailed back. '*What are you frightened of? S xx*'

I mean it's strange and new to be with someone who is like he is with me. He actually wants to connect, and I don't know if I can. It was easier when he was away. He was writing me those emails and it was all so dreamy, and I thought I was falling in love. Now I don't know if I feel anything for him at all. I don't know how I'm supposed to know. But I want to. I really want to.

E xx

Why not just stick with it for now? You've got to start somewhere, haven't you? I know what you mean, but it's great to try. It's really great. And it's OK if it doesn't work out.

BTW, I keep meaning to tell you about Tom's first swimming lesson. I looked away for one second and he just wandered over and jumped in! That was what I saw when I turned back round. His little body just disappearing off the edge, no water wings, nothing. It was terrifying. I mean, he was fine, they pulled him straight out, but you should have seen him. He was so proud of himself. It was so awful but so funny at the same time. He thinks he can swim just because he's seen other boys swimming.

I think that's what you have to do here, love. I know you're still hurting but you're going to have to hold your breath and jump in. I'll pull you out if it doesn't work. I'll always pull you out, OK?

S xxx

On Saturday afternoon, before I set off, I texted Susie and Magali his address.

Not 100% sure but think I might sleep at his place ... Only thing is he's still refusing to let me pay for anything, which is super-weird. So I might not. But if I do, here's my last known whereabouts ...

Over tea with Robert, I told him there was something that had been bothering me.

He nodded. 'Hit me with it. Whatever it is, sweetie, I'll put your mind at rest.'

I pointed out that since our first meeting he'd paid for every single thing we'd eaten and drunk, and that whenever I'd tried to take a turn, he hadn't let me.

'But I have more money than you. Possibly a lot more.' He ran his fingers through his thick, dark hair, and flashed a grin.

'You have no idea of my finances.'

'OK, then I just want to pay. It's what I do when I eat out, whoever I'm with.'

'Why?'

'It's just a rule.'

'Who says?'

'I do.'

'Well, if you want to keep seeing me it's a rule you'll have to break. We take it in turns. That's what people do.'

'Who?'

'Everyone I know. I don't want to be in debt to you.'

'OK,' he laughed. 'Let me talk to you about trade and exchange. It's like this: you do something for me, I do something for you. It's what makes us human. In fact, I'd say it's the single most important difference between humans and dogs. For us, it's the founding principle of modern society. For a Jack Russell, and I happen to know this, it's something they can't even comprehend.'

'Excuse me?'

'Wait, wait. I know it sounds bizarre, but literally, it's an indisputable fact.'

'How?'

'Listen to me. I tried it on Bella.'

'Who?'

'Our family dog. After Lena asked to separate, Bella and I spent a whole lot of time together. She's a Jack Russell. A beautiful creature. I moved into our basement, which was basically a separate kind of apartment. It was for our friends to stay in when they visited but Bella loved it down there, so we got to know each other pretty well. She just didn't get it. Two months, I tried. She never gave me a single thing in return. I gave her a tummy rub, she took it, and waltzed off. I gave her a ball, she gave me nothing back apart from the ball. I gave her a handful of treats, she —'

'So,' I interrupted, trying very hard to hide my complete amazement at what he was telling me, 'what's our trade here? You buy me food, I screw you?'

'That's not what I'm saying.'

'I'm your date, Robert, not your hooker.'

'Look, honey. Here's the thing. I'm going to carry on paying. So all we need to do is define your commodity. Simple.'

'I don't need to define my commodity. We're on a date.'

'Let me ask you a question.'

'Shoot.'

'What single thing do you wish you had more of?'

'Time. Always time.'

He sat back and raised a finger, slowly. 'Aha! That's our answer.'

'I'm sorry?'

'Time,' he said, staring at me. 'You're giving me your time. When you let me buy you dinner, that's your trade.'

'Doesn't work.'

'Because?'

'Because you're giving me *your* time too.'

'But I've got plenty to spare! If I'm not working, or with you, then I'm likely folding my socks or watching *Dexter*.

I'm alone. I'm lonely. Whatever you say, you're not going to win this one, so you're going to have to find a way to deal with it.'

'Or just not see you again.'

'Don't be mad at me. There's another way to look at this. It's the ships-crossing-paths rule.'

'The what?'

'I'm on starboard tack. I'm approaching you. You give way. It's just how it is. I have right of way.'

Robert knew the rules of the sea as well as another man might know his alphabet. The boat he'd sailed for twenty years around Maine and its islands belonged to his wife's mother. He'd managed and looked after the *Osedda* all that time, but by the time he met me, he'd handed it back to his mother-in-law.

That summer, he was planning to charter a different boat and sail with Philippe into Woods Hole, at Maine, where they'd visit his sister and her movie producer husband. Because Philippe was inexperienced, he'd stop off further up the coast and collect Charlotte's oldest boy, who knew the currents and tides and would pilot them in.

Winter evenings while I was at his desk on the half-landing, chasing the long-passed deadline for my new book, I'd look down to see him hunched over *Eldridge's Tide and Pilot*, or *Chapman Piloting & Seamanship*. At dinner once, he told me what slack-tide was, and that he'd discovered it wouldn't happen in daylight hours. He'd have to wait out the strongest of the ebbs and floods by standing off the ledges until just after dawn. Then he'd move away silently, with this small boy at the helm, holding a lantern and calling.

That afternoon at Tate Modern, I said that if he wouldn't let me pay for our tea, we'd have to say farewell.

I picked up my coat, and he put his hand on my arm.

'Whoa there. Whoa,' he said. 'Just hear me out, before you walk away. I'm gonna tell you a story, OK?'

We were the only people in the cafe. The waiter was hovering. Outside, the dark was falling. As he began, I sat back down.

In his late teens, using various means, he had travelled across Spain. Hitching rides and catching trains, he'd fallen in with a group of fellow adventurers, all young Americans like himself.

One evening, the group had gone to a restaurant. They were given a long table on the terrace, and spoke on and off with the *dueño*, who came out to see them especially, and made recommendations. They ate well, and were surprised when, reaching into their knapsacks to pool together funds, he reappeared and refused their money.

'You come to my country, I am your host,' he had declared flamboyantly. 'I come to yours, you invite me to dine with you in your homes.'

Several of the group had handed over their addresses, or their parents' addresses, pledging to reciprocate his generosity. Robert was so struck by this random act of generosity, and by the romance of the evening and the warm scent of almond blossom on the air, and the happiness of his compatriots, he had resolved there and then to be that man, always. To be the *dueño* in any gathering, and pay the bill whoever he was with.

Over tea at Tate Modern we came to an agreement of sorts. He said that if I felt left out, and wanted to thank him for dinner, I could buy him presents. I told him what he'd surmised about our relative finances was true: I was on a writer's budget. All of my writer and musician friends were in the same position, and rather than meeting in restaurants we more often cooked for one another at home. If it mattered to him to be able to take me out from time to time, then he could. But only occasionally, and as long as we spent as many evenings in, cooking for one another, or together.

'Like your Spanish host pronounced,' I said, 'I will invite you to my country, and you can dine with me.'

I have a collection of receipts from the six months we were together.

I picked up the first by accident, gathering my things from a restaurant table. As our relationship went on, I did it more consciously: on the application of his trade-and-exchange principle, I became fascinated by the question of what my time was costing him. When cracks began to form, and the end point came into view, I applied myself to the task assiduously, wanting to calculate precisely how much, in pots of hollandaise, and glasses of white burgundy, and ramekins of twice-baked soufflé, and scallops sautéed with pancetta, and wilted spinach, and mousse au chocolat, and crème brûlée, I was worth.

Looking through my collection, I found a bill from a brasserie we'd visited in Oxford one weekend. It was A4-sized, on thick cream paper. He'd drawn a graph on the back while we'd finished our coffee. The horizontal axis was labelled 'Years of Intimacy/Domesticity', and the vertical, 'Occurrence'.

With a black felt-tip pen, he had plotted the rising and falling of certain categories, including 'kissing frequency', 'kissing duration' and 'hand-holding'. The only line that rose over the years of intimacy and domesticity was the one for 'walking speed'. In my box file marked 'ROBERT', this graph lies on top of his family tree, with its angular lines and its stick men and women, and under his Venn diagram.

As we left the cafe the doors were being locked. We walked across the Millennium Bridge, with the lights on the water, then we decided to walk on and see what we found. We neared the bars of Smithfield, where I often went with Magali, and I asked him if he'd like a drink.

'I'm not much of a drinker,' he said, shaking his head. 'You must've noticed on our dates. I'll keep you company, though, if you're thirsty.'

Downstairs at Smiths, he ordered me a cocktail, and mineral water for himself. There was music, and he made me laugh with his stories. We flirted until he said, 'Shall we? Can we?' Under the table, he took my hand. He put his other hand lightly between my legs, sliding it higher, then he said, 'Will you please come home with me?'

At his place, he showed me the code for the gates, 'For next time.' Inside, he stopped on the red-brick stairs and lifted me into his arms and wrapped my legs around him and began to kiss me. In his apartment, he set me down.

'Oh, wait,' he said. 'Is it warm enough for you in here?'

'Yes. What's wrong? It's OK if you don't −'

'I do.' He put a hand on my lower back. 'You wanna take a look around first?'

'OK,' I said, surprised.

We got as far as the mezzanine, then I took off my sweater and he unzipped his flies and we fell onto a sofa and it began properly, on a fur throw with me on top of him until he lifted me and wrapped me in the fur throw and carried me down and we finished it in bed and when he came he roared and juddered like a ship or a killer whale. When it stopped, I thought I might be crushed by the weight and the strength of him, or that my ears might have been pierced by his roar. He lay on me, panting, until I tapped his shoulder and said, 'Honey, you're –'

'Am I too heavy?'

'You're too heavy,' and he rolled off.

We lay half under half over the sheets while his breathing steadied. Then, in the darkness, he told me a story.

Just after Lena asked for their separation, he travelled to New Zealand on business.

In Auckland, he visited the museum and went to the volcano gallery. Finding himself in a mocked-up living room, complete with slatted blinds, lamps and a coffee table, he took an armchair and watched the TV that was playing in the corner.

A news anchorwoman was partway through reporting that the city was waiting, having received a warning that a volcanic eruption might take place imminently. Footage of gridlocked traffic was shown, intercut with clips of angry residents being interviewed. They had been advised to leave but couldn't.

The mocked-up living room had a large window to the left of the television, with a view that matched the one from Robert's hotel: the bay around the city, a calm flat ocean. The anchorwoman interviewed an expert who explained quite calmly what would be the first sign of an eruption beginning. Just as he described the low, flat cloud of ash that would appear on the surface of the water, such a cloud emerged from the ocean outside the window and, almost imperceptibly, spread.

The expert continued: once the cloud had appeared and started moving, there was no escape.

The atmosphere in the living room changed. A child climbed onto her mother's lap. The anchorwoman interrupted the interview.

'We are going to go live to our –' she said, and the expert confirmed: the eruption had begun.

Through the window Robert saw an explosion rise from the water. There was the sound of glass shattering and the TV shook from side to side. The cloud became a mushroom cloud, with black ash rising through it, and the TV short-circuited.

The lights in the mocked-up living room flickered then went out. Someone in the room cried, then there was silence.

Robert went to his hotel, where he spent the rest of the day in bed.

'I literally couldn't move,' he said to me quietly. 'I mean, I just lay there in total darkness. I had no idea who I was.'

Throughout his story, I hadn't said a word.

He slept for a half-hour and I watched the rain on the windows. Then he woke, and I asked for something to eat. I was hungry, I said, really hungry, so he dialled for sushi and ordered double.

We stayed in bed and made love. When the sushi arrived, we ate at his breakfast bar, feeding each other first, then ourselves.

I told him he was the first guy I'd ever gone home with who had tried to show me his place before having sex.

'I wanted you to feel safe,' he said. 'I wanted you to know your exits and entrances. I wanted to make sure you were warm! I wanted –'

'Hey. I was teasing.' Then I undid his robe.

He moved the sushi boxes, and said, 'Shall we try without?'

'Without what?'

'A condom.'

'Are you kidding?'

'They're kind of, you know.'

'Kind of what?'

'I don't like them.'

'I've only just met you. No condom, no sex.'

'Oh,' he said, then he got one and rolled it on, frowning, and we made love on the breakfast bar.

In bed again, we fell asleep until his breathing woke me. It was quiet, like the breathing of a small cat. It didn't exactly disturb me, but when the upstairs neighbour's dog began to run around, I couldn't get back to sleep.

I wrapped myself in his shirt and found the fur throw on the floor. It was heavy, and lined with silk. I took it to the mezzanine and switched on the lamp. The bookcases were pristine, the books in height order; there were some travel guides, two copies of *How to Invest Wisely*, and some great American novels. There was a volume about Swedish ceramics, and a geopolitical history of the world.

On the desk was an iPad, and a single sharpened pencil. The shelf to the left of the desk was empty, but for a single framed photo. For anyone using the desk, the image was at eye level: a very young woman, holding a baby. The frame was carved from mahogany, the woman's face was soft and pink. I turned the photo the other way and switched off the lamp, then I lay on the sofa under the throw, and slept.

When I opened my eyes he was standing over me. 'Did I snore?'

'Only a little.'

'Did I wake you? Is that why you're up here?'

'It's fine. There was a dog in the apartment upstairs. That's what woke me. Then I heard you and couldn't sleep, just because, you know.'

'I woke up on my own and I thought you'd gone.'

'No, honey.' I reached out my arms. 'I was here. I was sleeping.'

The fur-silk throw, he would tell me later when I admired it, had been made by a small company Lena had set up when the family lived in Tokyo. She was bored, he said: there was a nanny for Philippe, and a cook, and someone to look after the house. So she'd started the business, which dealt in luxury gifts for the home.

Other objects that had been made by Lena's company would emerge in the time we were together. A ceramic vase, candlesticks carved from sandalwood, and the mahogany photo frame, with its picture of Lena and Philippe.

I liked the throw most of all. In those early days, it didn't bother me at all to discover it came from her, this throw we had made love on the first time. It was heavy and warm and had a scent I couldn't identify but which smelled feminine to me, in a husky kind of a way. Once, when I was wrapped in it and we were watching *The Unbearable Lightness of Being* on DVD, I turned to find Robert staring at me.

'What?'

'I'm watching you.'

'I know. Why?'

'I want to see what you're feeling. I want to know what to feel.'

In bed again that first time, he laid me on top of the sheet. Then he went down on me, with his whole big face and his mouth. I came, then we slept until nearly midday when he woke me and said, what did I want for breakfast?

'Anything,' I said. 'As long as it involves coffee.'

He went across the street, and brought back a tray of coffee, and pastries called 'cronuts'. He was amazed by them, as though someone had invented the wheel for the first time and given it him for free. He said he'd got a kick out of standing at the counter knowing he smelled of me.

'I wonder if they guessed,' he said, grinning like a kid, and raising his left eyebrow. 'I didn't even wash my face. They must've.' He set the coffees down and slid the sheet from me and laid his face on my belly.

'Hey, wait,' I said. 'Can I have a coffee? I really need coffee.'

He asked me questions the whole day through. I answered hardly any of them in detail, and when he complained 'I need to know you', I reminded him we'd only just met, and said it was good that he didn't.

I kissed him. 'Desire depends on not knowing too much, doesn't it?' I kissed him again. 'Anyhow, I have to go.'

'Where?'

'To a birthday party.'

Robert pulled a pretend frown. 'Am I coming too?'

'Are you coming where?'

'To the party?'

'No.'

'Why not?'

'Because it's a surprise dinner for a good friend's birthday. We've been planning it for ages, way before I met you.'

'So? I don't mind.'

'So it would be very, very weird. None of them know you. Why would you want to, anyway?'

'OK,' he said, 'OK,' but I could tell he didn't get it.

He found a piece of paper and his iPad, and asked for the address. By the time I'd showered, he had written out my route and my options from Angel station.

I still have that piece of paper. Looking at it now, I can see his crestfallen little-boy face as he handed it me and tried one last time. 'Are you sure you need to go on your own?'

'I'm sure.'

He had used his black felt tip. The nib was flat, rather than pointed, and the ink had nearly run dry, so some of the letters have faded a little. His script is all capitals and the text is set in blocks, with stylised arrows that are flared to their edges.

The piece of paper is torn from a sketchbook he'd proudly shown me that morning, while we'd drunk our takeaway coffee and eaten our cronuts. The sketchbook contained his small watercolours of a trip he'd taken with a group of his and Lena's friends, along the Danube. The spare page he'd torn from it, for my route, was small and rectangular, the paper heavy and expensive.

He'd written the Tube line (though there's only one from Angel), the name of the destination station, and after that, all six onward bus numbers for me to choose between. The numbers fell in a perfect column, aligned to the right as though the paper was a grid, its boxes filled in by an accountant.

When I left his apartment I was late and had to run. On the Tube platform, I reached in my pocket and held the piece of paper in my hand.

'Safe,' I said out loud. 'I feel safe.'

After the dinner, my friends and I made our birthday toasts to Magali. Then we lay back on big floor cushions drinking wine, and they asked about my dark-haired American.

'You know the craziest thing?' I said, when I'd told them about him.

'That you made him take you on three dates before you fucked him?' Magali called out.

'Funny. Thanks. No, actually. It's that this morning when we woke up he asked me –'

'Nothing X-rated please,' Olivier said, laughing.

'He asked me if I wanted kids.'

Our friends laughed, or howled and rolled their eyes. 'What did you say?'

'I said I couldn't answer the question in the abstract.'

'And?'

'And I asked him it back. He said he couldn't rule it out. But that he thought it unlikely. That he loves his son and he doesn't ever want to be half a father to him. That there's a twelve-year age gap between us which is the same as the age gap between his parents. That his mum likely cheated on his dad and that could be a problem with a younger woman and –'

The laughing was too loud. I listened, then I said, 'Yeah, OK, look. This guy was married for twenty years. He just got dumped. Yes, he's new to dating. Yes, he was lonely when he met me. Yes, he's a bit weird but he's kind of sweet, and he did dial out for sushi in the middle of the night, and he did bring me breakfast in bed.'

'And tried to invite himself to Magali's party, and made you give him the address!' Olivier said.

There was more laughter, and I tried to defend him: it hadn't been at all difficult to refuse him; he'd accepted being told no, straight away.

'I should hope so, sweetheart,' Magali declared. 'How old did you say he is? You really want gramps checking up on you every time you go to something without him?'

The next time we slept together, he woke me with breakfast, and returned to the subject of children. Again, it struck me as absurd, but this time I made an effort to be more open. Yes, I said, I wanted a child one day, with someone.

In response, he talked about himself, and about Philippe. I kept silent while he talked, and didn't tell him that I had nearly had a daughter.

That my husband and I were going to call her Phoebe.

That we had longed for her. Imagined her. Seen her as a little person on her scans, and seen her life unfolding.

That, when we were told it was all over, my husband had wept in front of the obstetrician, and that I still wept over the fact she'd not stayed long enough to be born, and that, in the end, when we'd tried again and failed again, and the sadness had been too much, we had parted. That now, four years on, he had found someone new to fall in love with and make a home with, but that I had not and thought I would never be able to. But that deep inside me, stitched into my soul, was a longing so strong it frightened me.

Having kept silent that morning in bed, I listened to Robert's tales of fatherhood. What came next took me by surprise, and when he was done, it was with a sense of unreality that I agreed to his proposal.

We would continue to see each other.

We would be aware of the difficulties our age gap presented, and try to work with them not against them.

I would visit my doctor and talk about other forms of contraception, which might allow him more pleasure than condoms.

In return, he made a promise: if, at any point, he found that he'd reached a firm decision as to whether he wanted to become a father again, he would tell me immediately. He would not let me stay on false pretences. If he knew his answer to be no, he would set me free to find someone else. For now, we agreed, the question would remain suspended.

I saw my GP that week, while Robert was in Canada.

She listened to my story, then she told me Robert would just have to manage with condoms. Time was short, she advised. There was no point going on the pill and off again, if one day I wanted to conceive. If I became aware he wasn't the man for me, or if he told me he did not, in fact, want children, I should walk away double quick and give my eggs to someone who did.

He emailed from Calgary.

> *I'm thinking about how I found you upstairs the first night.*
>
> *I climb up, and in the blue gloom just manage to see you, balled up under the throw. I am grateful that you're there, but I also suddenly worry that you will be furious at being kept awake. Then your arms stretch out towards me and undulate like the tentacles of some improbable sea anemone, lined with cnidocytes. There is a beautiful polyp in my house! You draw me close and capture me. I am so relieved.*

The same thing happened as had happened when I'd received his emails from Mexico. Something in me unfroze a little further, and I fell a tiny bit more in love. This time, though, the feeling was too big, and I didn't know what to do with it.

I wrote that I would interpret his comments as playful, romantic expressions of the complex nature of attraction and desire, and of the conflicts any man might feel arising between his need to want a woman, and to be wanted by her.

> *And because I am letting myself go with whatever this situation is, I'll set aside the fact that polyps are something one usually seeks to have surgically removed and that cnidocytes are toxic weapons, designed to entrap or to maim or to kill.*
>
> *Come back soon, stranger.*

He called from the airport. He asked about my week, what I'd done while he was away.

'I emailed. I told you already.'

'But there were no specifics.'

'Nothing really happened.'

'Something must've happened. Anything. I don't mind what. Tell me anything.'

'OK. I saw my GP.'

'Really?'

'Really.'

'What'd she say?'

I was relating parts of the doctor's recommendations when he jumped in. 'I can't believe you count that as "nothing"! That's definitely not nothing. It's definitely something.'

'OK,' I said. 'OK.' Then I asked when he'd be back, and whether he wanted to see me.

'Of course. Come over tonight.'

'It'll be late. You'll be tired. We can leave it.'

'Come whenever,' he said. 'I want to see you. I want to hold you.'

'Before 10.30 then. If I can't be there by 10.30, I won't.'

He let me in and took my bag and my coat. Standing just inside the door, he said, 'Hold out your hands. I got you a present.'

He gave me a small, pearl-white cardboard box. On the lid were the words 'The diamond standard in thinness: crystal clear (microfine), latex-free'.

'If I'm going to abide by your lady doctor's instructions, I'll do it in style.'

He put his hands over my eyes and led me through to the living space. When I looked, I saw that he'd filled the whole of the lower floor of his apartment with tiny candles.

Thinking back now, I realise there must have been one, two hundred of the things, and I wonder how long it would have taken, and what he was thinking as he crouched there, bringing each flame to life.

The blinds were thrown up. In the darkness, with just those little candles, the space seemed even bigger than it was. Cocooned in that sea of light, I felt wanted. He had put the bedspread on the floor and he led me to it and undressed me very slowly. He hardly said a word and we knelt and placed our hands on one another, then we lay down together and there was the scent of sandalwood and the warmth from the flames and from his skin.

February

One of the most common troubles that a sculler experiences is the discovery that his boat will not run straight. For example, the left scull may seem to have a tendency to pull the boat round. It is not the fault of the boat or the sculls, and if another sculler were to try the boat he might find an opposite tendency. It may be due to several causes; the sculler has probably developed a habit of looking over this shoulder when he turns to sight his course.

A. Eggar, *Rowing and Sculling*

He said the words before I'd thought them.

'How can you?' I responded. 'You know less than nothing about me.'

'What else can I call it? I'm in love. I love you.'

'Those are two different things.'

'What else am I supposed to do with these feelings?' He smiled lazily.

It was the first weekend he'd stayed over at my place. In the morning he took a photo of us on his phone to email to his sister, then he held me in closer to take another photo and I said, 'No, please, I just woke up. My hair.'

We were leaving when he asked me to wait. I watched him open my kitchen cupboards, one by one. He picked up every pot and jar and box and carton, turning them in his hands and replacing them.

When I next visited him I found the contents replicated in his own cupboards. Every foodstuff I possessed had been given a double. From that point on, there were my oats for my breakfast, my tea for my tea. I spread my own acacia honey on my toast every morning. There were peppermint infusions before I slept, and satsumas. For snacks there were carrots, and for dinner sometimes, without my having asked, there were pieces of tenderstem broccoli, or petits pois, with beurre d'Isigny and rough sea salt.

The second time he stayed at my flat he brought three shirts. While he was showering for work, I put them back in his bag. A few days on, he brought them again and I let him find a drawer for them, saying I was impressed by his ironing and he was welcome to do mine.

'I can't take the credit, honey,' he laughed.

The woman who had done his shirts came to his apartment once a week, and spent all day there. For the whole eight years that the family had lived in London, Mimi had been what he called their 'housekeeper'. When Philippe was young, Robert told me, it had been Mimi's occasional habit to stay the night, if he and Lena were out.

Eventually they gave her a bedroom in the eaves of the house, to save her coming and going late at night, or early in the morning.

She had become, he said, part of the family.

When he moved to his apartment, he'd asked if she could be spared once a week. With Philippe away at college, and Lena living in her flat in Primrose Hill that, while sizeable, was nowhere near as big as the house had been, she couldn't object.

'It's fine,' he said, when I asked him if it was awkward. 'We share her.'

Because we never met, I came to think of Mimi as an emissary, this woman who arrived direct from Lena's flat to clear away Robert's dishes and his used condoms and once, when I had my period, to empty the bathroom bin and leave a roll of small paper bags next to it.

One Saturday, we took a day trip to Brighton. Coming out of the station, I waited by the news-stand while he called her.

'You phone your cleaner at the weekend?'

'She's not "my cleaner". I had a missed call. There was a problem with her keys. Or with her mother in Hong Kong. Or something. I just asked for more details but she wouldn't say. Lena will know. I'll find out when I go over for my mail.'

'Lena gets your post?'

'Yep.'

'Why?'

'We did a joint change of address to her new place.'

'Why?'

'Simpler.'

Two years on from my divorce, I bought a new address book. The one it replaced was a glossy ring-bound hardback, with an oil painting on its front (*At the Gallery* by Paul Gustav) and a pert-breasted Gauguin on its back. A gift from my parents when we'd first moved in together, it was a palimpsest of our marriage: with alternate pages carrying prints or oils or portraits from the National Gallery, its lined facing pages recorded, by way of our crossings-out and rewritings, every relocation and birth and death and new relationship among our friends, and families.

When I'd asked to take the book, my ex-husband had photocopied a few pages and, without objecting, let it go.

In the two, maybe three years that followed our separation, writing Christmas cards or acknowledging birthdays, it was his cursive I found more often than my own. Knowing that, I'd pause before opening it, and stare at Gustav's well-dressed Edwardian couple on the cover. They clutched gallery guides and stood over a wall-full of prints, so it wasn't possible to see their expressions or know if they were happy or sad.

Then one spring morning, taking a shortcut through an Oxford Street department store, I passed a shelf of stationery and my eye was caught by a smaller, brighter book. Covered in a soft, papery fabric, it had only lined cream pages inside. That evening I opened the old address book. Transcribing some of the pages and abandoning others, I re-charted the map of my life.

When Robert said that he collected his post from Lena, I wanted to tell him to stop.

I wanted to say that by changing his address, he would be taking a step towards thinking of himself as separate from that former, shared life, but that by continuing to report in to her, and allowing her to take receipt of everything that came to him from the outside world, he was in no way free, nor would he ever be.

Instead, I only gently questioned their arrangement.

Abruptly, he told me the system suited him: it gave them a reason to check in on each other, and gave Robert an excuse to see Bella, who had been his dog after all, more than she'd been Lena's.

When you're starting out with someone new, who for twenty years was married to the mother of his child, how do you navigate the space she left behind?

He pronounced her name 'Lay-nah'.

I'd read about her even before I'd met Robert. In the eighth Google hit for his name, the word WEDDING stood out in bold capitals. Searching beyond that announcement, I discovered she'd written a book about Swedish porcelain. On her publisher page, she used her name and his, without a hyphen. I could find only a couple of images: one of them showed her bestowing a medal on behalf of her mother's charitable foundation; another, her arrival at a party for the launch of a New York fashion magazine.

In the only dream I had of her she wore a pale green silk jacket, cut high on her neck. Her hair was blonde and straight. She wore it long with a blunt-cut fringe that was almost to her eyes.

Turning her gaze on me, she undid her jacket.

The skin of her torso fell in soft, puckered folds like the layer that forms on a pan of milk, just before it reaches boiling point. Her breasts were flat pouches, falling towards her waist.

She looked at me a little longer, then she fastened her jacket and turned away.

Beyond the online ghost trail, I had only his stories to go on.

In the summer of their first meeting, Robert was back and forth between London and New York. Lena had started a master's at London University and was living with her English boyfriend. Initially, Robert waged his campaign by post. It didn't matter *what* he sent, he explained, only that an envelope or a package landed on her doormat daily, bearing her name and address in Robert's handwriting, and on the reverse, his own. Within a few weeks he had persuaded her to be unfaithful. By the autumn she was living in New York as Robert's wife, already pregnant with Philippe.

If the story of those daily deliveries struck me as the stuff of revisionist fantasy, his descriptions of the years immediately prior to our meeting were more credible. Because their north London house stood in a street I knew and had often walked down, I could picture their comings and goings as though they were friends of friends, or neighbours.

The house, which was red-brick and Victorian, was almost as wide as it was tall. Robert had met the monthly rent (which he called 'sizeable') partly from his salary and partly from his savings. He told me he agreed with Lena that this arrangement was fair: it was his career which had brought them back to London, after all. Since abandoning her master's, Lena's sources of income had been twofold: a monthly payment from her mother's trust fund, and the rent on a Manhattan brownstone, which she and Robert had bought in her name. Recently, she had spoken of completing the master's and seeing about a career of her own, now that Philippe had finished school.

There were the vacations, though, which Robert said Lena was reluctant to give up.

'Would doing a master's stop her going on holiday?' I'd asked him. 'How many did you take?'

'Let's just say, a lot.'

'Really? What about your work?'

'I took it with me. Or fixed meetings nearby, or dialled in to a conference call, you know.'

'Not really.'

'Anyhow, she couldn't really have done any serious study, travelling that often.'

'Where did you go?' I'd asked. As if he'd known I was wondering about the cost, he said the deal they had struck was simple: for winter trips in Connecticut or Zermatt, and summer ones in Sweden or Maine, Lena saw to the accommodation by selecting a property from her mother's portfolio, gratis. Easters and half-terms were with friends of hers at their properties in the Stockholm archipelago, the south of France or the Aegean. In all seasons, Robert was responsible for their travel arrangements, which Lena preferred to be first class.

'Did you ever suggest economy?'

'She was open to it in principle,' Robert said, 'but in practice, you know.'

'In practice, what?'

'There were other people involved.'

'Which other people?'

'Our friends. We had to travel how they travelled. Be friendly. Lena was always very careful about other people.'

During their London years there were three dinners a week, more often four. At a certain point in the afternoon,

Lena would message him a restaurant and a time. If it was a smart place, and she felt what he'd worn to work that morning wasn't quite right, she'd courier him a shirt or a suit. Often, their dinner companions were new to him and he made sure to be on time. Occasionally, though, if he had notice of the guest list and particularly disliked someone on it, he would feign a conference call and be late.

'Why did you go at all?'

'Duty. It was a couples thing, you know.'

With one of the couples, whose son had been a classmate of Philippe's, it was their custom to have dinner then see a play. The father, Brad, was unusual in Lena's circle for having a salaried job.

'Didn't have a lot of time for the guy, but at least we had something to talk about. Work, I mean. And cycling. We could talk about bicycles and offices. It was fine.'

On alternate outings, either Lena or Chrissy chose the play, and the other booked a restaurant. Robert and Brad simply had to show up, and take it in turns to pay.

Robert told me once that Brad had been emailing about their cycling club and added that Chrissy had tickets for Fiona Shaw's *The Testament of Mary*. They'd heard news of a girlfriend, and wondered if she'd like to take Lena's place? It was Brad's turn to pay for dinner, he'd written; it would be his pleasure to host the happy couple.

'How much are the tickets?' I asked.

'It's fine.'

'But how much?'

'Doesn't matter. You'd be doing me a favour by coming. Chrissy will reserve a restaurant.'

At a bistro on Whitecross Street, before we'd quite sat down, Brad asked us to order as quickly as possible: the pre-theatre menu was only available until 6.30. Making his recommendations, he signalled to the waiter. When I asked for more time, Brad shook his head and began to order for me. I laughed.

'What's funny?' Robert said.

'Brad is.' I glanced at Brad, then I smiled at Robert and Chrissy. 'He's trying to choose for me. Don't worry,' I said, turning back to Brad. 'There's nothing I want on the pre-theatre,' then I asked the waiter for another five minutes.

In the morning, Robert asked why I'd switched to the à la carte.

'I had a salad,' I said. 'It was pretty much the same price as the pre-theatre. Anyway Brad's a hedge fund manager. What does he care?'

'It's not the price, honey. Why didn't you just do what he wanted?'

'Because it wasn't what *I* wanted.'

'But that's not how it's done.'

'How what's done?'

'Dinner with friends.'

'They're not friends. When I placed my order they were virtual strangers. This morning I'd be prepared to go as far as calling them acquaintances. Hang on, Robert. That's not "how it's done". Not with my friends, that's for sure. Anyway, you don't even like them.'

'I never said that.'

'You did. You said you hated going and you only ever did it for Lena. It was your duty.'

'So doesn't that count for you, now?'

'No! Even if I *was* under a duty to you, whatever that means, it certainly wouldn't extend to letting Brad tell me what to eat. Do you realise the only thing he talked about for the entire meal, while you were attempting to flirt with Chrissy, was how much he sold his Arsenal season ticket for?'

'So?'

'Why would he think that was interesting?'

'It's trading. That's his business. He's very good at it.'

'So what was all the "order-by-6.30-or-I'll-order-for-you" fiasco? He would've saved approximately £2.50. Did you notice what he did when Fiona Shaw came on stage?'

'What?'

'He carried on talking.'

'He did not.'

'Did. At the beginning, I mean. When the lights were still up and she appeared from nowhere. She was so amazing. She stood completely still. Like a statue. Then she walked around like a, like a – she looked like an *actual* wraith. A ghost. The whole auditorium went quiet. Except Brad. He continued with his explanation of the Enron crisis.'

'Enron was a pretty big deal, honey.'

'So is the mother of Christ, especially played by Fiona Shaw. Your man was the only person not watching her like a hawk. And when the lights *did* go down, you know what he did?'

'What?'

'He fell asleep!'

'How do you know?'

'He snored! His head lolled over, practically on my shoulder. I can understand why you were dreading the evening. Why not just say no?'

'You didn't seem too unhappy when we got back.'

'What?'

'You were hot, honey. You were undressing me before we got in the apartment.'

'I was a bit drunk, and very, very frustrated. Sorry to break it to you, but you could've been just about anyone.'

The evening with Brad and Chrissy was the only time Robert asked me so directly to step into Lena's role. Later, he would be more subtle, so I'd discover during the course of an evening that I was there by proxy.

The one occasion when he strayed into my married past, he did so uninvited.

When I mentioned to Robert I'd been asked to give a reading at my old friend Stefano's college in Cambridge and would stay over after the dinner, he asked straight away where I'd sleep.

'Stefano's booked me a college room,' I said. 'It'll be fun.'

'That's crazy. I'll find us a hotel. We can make a weekend of it. I have friends in Cambridge, too. Haven't seen them in a while, seriously. I'll take them for dinner while you're with your academics, then you and I can spend the night.'

I thanked him for his invitation, then I explained that there had never been any sexual attraction between Stefano and me.

'OK. So how do you even know the guy?'

'He was a colleague of my husband's. It was a long, long time ago. We were good friends, all of us. He's still a friend of mine. It's that simple.'

'You've never told me about him.'

'I've only known you two months. There are plenty of things you have yet to discover. Look. We're practically family. I'm his daughter's godmother. He's avuncular. That's how he's always been with me. I'll be back in town by Saturday lunchtime, you and I can start our weekend then.'

Just before I left for Cambridge, Robert emailed me the hotel reservation. He had booked a "Rooftop Suite", with a view.

'*It's not every weekend I get to take a literary superstar away,*' he wrote.

Already late for my train, I didn't reply.

Gently rotund, and cherubic, Stefano had walked us to our wedding ceremony. In time, we had read bedtime stories to his daughter in her nursery, and carved pumpkins with her at Halloween. Though our friendship was recast by my break-up, for me he would always be that earlier Stefano.

At Cambridge, I met him in the station forecourt and told him I didn't need the guest room after all.

'What?' he laughed. 'You're propositioning me? After all these years I'm finally getting the green light?'

I laughed too. When I explained that Robert had booked us into a hotel, Stefano flicked his eyebrows up, then down, twice, but said it was no problem. Leaving the station, I saw him frown.

'Is that how it works with you two, Elizabeth? Robert's your papa, now?'

'I think he might be a little jealous.'

'Of what?'

'Of you.'

'Ha!' Stefano shouted. 'Ha ha ha ha ha ha ha!' He doubled over, blocking the pavement so people had to step into the street to get past. He laughed so loud I put my hands over my ears. He held his midriff and carried on laughing, like I remembered him doing with my husband. I put my bag down and I listened. I wanted to cry it made me so happy and sad at the same time, to be brought back sharp.

Later, before the hall doors were opened for my reading, he told me to be careful.

'A guy who does that, you know. It can be a problem.'

'What sort of a problem?'

'Tell me, my dear, sweet Elizabeth. Does he make you happy?'

'Happy how? What kind of happy?'

'Happy like you used to be. When we were younger, all of us.'

'I'll never be happy like that again, will I? Not how I was then. So, what can I say? It's a difficult question.'

'Is it?'

'My horizons have changed.'

'Is he good to you?'

'He's good in the way he knows how to be.'

'Is it the way you want?'

'I don't want to be on my own again.'

'Even this evening? You don't want to be without him now, here with your old friend Stefano?'

'I wanted to be on my own this evening, with this.' I gestured to the hall, the rows of chairs. 'And this,' I said, holding up the novel I would read from. 'And you, my old friend Stefano.' Then I grinned. 'So, will you mind when you hear my reading?'

'Why would I?'

'I chose the dirtiest scene I could find. Then I added some dirty stuff.'

'Ha!' he shouted, raising his eyebrows again. 'Ha ha ha ha ha ha ha!'

Someone opened the doors, and people were coming in, and Stefano was drying his eyes and I was laughing too and Robert was forgotten.

At the hotel later that night, he was tetchy.

'You didn't have to stay up,' I said.

'I wanted to.'

'So don't complain.'

I went to the bathroom. He called out, 'Are you getting undressed?'

'Yes.'

'Come back here. I wanna watch.'

As it happened, his dinner companions had cancelled. Alone in the oversized suite, he'd ordered room service and drunk coffee to stay awake. Walking back after Stefano's dinner, I'd followed the streets around the hotel for as long as I could, but still hadn't had time to absorb my evening. Then Robert was there, needing my attention, and my memories of that other life were silenced.

In bed, I pushed him away.

'We can fuck in the morning. I want to sleep.'

I waited until I heard his small-cat breathing. Getting up, I opened the curtains and remembered how, on the morning of my wedding, Stefano and my ex-husband had stood beneath the window of the room where Stefano's wife, Giulia, was helping me to dress. When we heard them call, we looked down and the two men sang a duet in Italian, something silly. At the wedding breakfast, Stefano opened a bottle of champagne and it splashed my dress a little and he sang again, '*Sposa bagnata, sposa fortunata.*' Everyone had laughed, and it was days before I'd understood the joke.

In the morning Robert asked me to put a pillow beneath my hips.

'It means I can go deeper. I think you'll like it.'

I didn't, but the physical sensations were intense enough to stop me feeling sad. Afterwards, I looked for the condom.

'Did you wear one?'

'You put it on me.'

'Did you keep it on, I mean?'

'Of course I did. Stay calm. It must be still inside you.'

'It's not.' I knelt up on the bed. I felt inside myself again. I was crying. 'It must've come out. It must've come off when you started. Or you took it off when you went in. I had my eyes closed. Where is it? Show me it.'

'Don't say that. I wouldn't do that. We made a deal.'

He got off the bed and started moving the pillows, the sheets. Then he knelt on the floor.

In the shower, I stood under the hot water and breathed too fast. I turned over the idea that I might be pregnant, and that that was what I wanted more than anything. Then straight away there was another idea, which was that Robert didn't make me happy in the way Stefano had described, and that the reason I hadn't been able to admit this to Stefano was that I was barely able to admit it to myself. Then I felt the condom slip out of me and slide down my leg to the shower floor. Picking it up, I squeezed it empty, then I dropped it in the bin.

It had been pushed, I supposed, right inside me. With my hips raised up on the pillow, he'd slid himself in and pressed with his full weight. When he'd come, he'd lain in me until he was limp, and it must have stayed there when he pulled out.

In London again, I bought a morning-after pill.

At the till, I hesitated, but there was Stefano's warning.

That evening, I helped Magali and Olivier at the club. When we were done they made coffee, and asked me about my weekend. I told them we'd walked to Grantchester, which was something I'd always wanted to do.

'He taught me how to stroke a horse,' I said. 'I've never done that before. I've seen them up close. But I've never touched one.'

'A new thing,' Olivier said.

'He showed me how to know if it was comfortable.'

'How?'

'You watch its ears. You can tell from how its ears are moving. It's not hard. You just have to know what to do. You have to trust they're going to like it, then you touch them.' At that field gate, I had felt the animal's warm breath on my hand and felt the same warmth in my stomach.

While Olivier was cashing up, Magali asked me, 'Any other new things?'

'Sex with my hips up on a pillow. Better for him than for me, I think.'

'It's good, the sex?'

'Usually. This was the first time I didn't like it. I mean, it was fine, kind of.'

'Any other new things?

'A vintage carpentry shop.'

'Carpentry? For sex?'

'No! For wooden things. Faux vintage. Tools. Domestic equipment. Antique-style dishwashing brushes, you know. Robert looked at the tools. He bought himself a lathe. I looked at toys.'

'What kind of toys?'

'For babies. And very small children. Wooden spinning tops, and rattles.'

'Did he look at them?'

'I tried to show him. It was as though he didn't see them. He doesn't want – You know, I know he doesn't. He's playing with me. He wasn't interested. He went back to the tools. He didn't want to look at children's toys.'

'Of course he doesn't, not yet. He's still thinking of different ways to have sex. Give it time.'

'How much? I want a child. When do I give up?'

'You'll know when.'

Coming out of the faux-vintage shop, we'd bumped into Stefano.

I was as delighted as him by the chance encounter. Disengaging from our embrace, I saw Robert's face darken. Stefano put out his hand and said, beginning to laugh, 'You must be Robert!'

Robert, keeping his hands behind his back, inclined his head. Raising it, he smiled, tightly.

London that night was just a stopover for Robert. I said goodbye without having told him about the morning-after pill. When I emailed him in Doha to tell him I was ill, he emailed straight back to ask why. I said it must have been something I'd eaten, or maybe I was just overtired. His reply, which came within minutes, attached a reservation for a massage.

Opening the link, I saw that it was a spa I'd walked past with Magali a hundred times, on the way to the club. The scent that came out onto the street, if someone was leaving as we passed, was heady and exotic. The massage he'd chosen for me was 'aromatherapeutic' and would take an hour. Within two seconds I'd compiled a list of reasons not to go. Trying to find a way to accept his kindness, I set aside the first three (I didn't have an hour to spare; I'd only ever had one massage in my life and it had hurt, terribly; I felt too ill to even get there) and looked at the description again. Then I thought of Magali and the black crêpe scarf, and of what she'd say if I didn't go.

After it was over, I took a bus home.

The woman sitting next to me woke me just before the bus reached my flat, laughing. I'd rested my head on her shoulder, she said. She didn't mind especially, but she'd been about to get off, and hadn't wanted to leave me sleeping, in case I missed my stop.

I ran a bath and emailed Robert to thank him. I wrote that it had made me feel more relaxed than I'd ever been, and I was about to take a long soak. He called just as I got in. We spoke for a half-hour, or rather he did, only letting me go when I'd answered all his questions about was it a full body massage, and had I undressed completely, and was the masseur male or female, and had I had one of those beds, he wanted to know, where you put your face on a padded ring and looked at the floor, and weren't they strange?

Before going to sleep that night, I opened the link again and read the price list. For the same amount of money, apparently, I could've paid a week's rent. I wrote again to thank him, and asked him not to call in the morning; I wanted to lie in. Falling asleep, I thought of my friends, and tried to decide which of them I'd do that for, if I was ever rich: send an email with a reservation at a smart London spa, telling them to take an hour off work, and be aromatherapeuterised.

Our respective financial situations were just as soon glanced at as they were glanced away from.

By the time I met Robert, I'd published some novels and had found a way of living which I was able to sustain. If I taught a little, marked papers a little, worked the occasional shift at Magali's and Olivier's, and had no expectation of owning a property, I could do what I wanted and spend most of my time writing.

When, at the end of January, I'd been told I had to move because my landlord was selling up, Robert had offered to help.

'You're leaving it so late,' he said in February, as the date neared and still I hadn't found anywhere. 'How can you just not know where you're going? It's two weeks away, honey. You've got to get ready.'

The first advert he forwarded me was for a one-room place in Primrose Hill. On the market for six times what I was paying, which was already a little too much, it was half the size of my place. Then a friend of a friend got in touch about a flat he owned on the Bethnal Green Road, not far from Victoria Park. I could see from the photos that although it was too small for all my things, it was right for me in every other way. We agreed a lower rent for the first few weeks, until I could find a flatmate to move in.

'You're taking it?' Robert said on the phone from Vienna one night. 'Just like that? Are you crazy? You haven't checked out anywhere else!'

'I don't need to.'

'Are you even going to —?'

'Of course I am. I've got a viewing Friday. I'll measure up, meet the neighbours, do all that stuff. Then if everything's OK, I'll sign. Wanna come? Will you be back by then? You could pretend to be my architect!'

When he played along with my game and asked me to email him the photos, I did, saying I would sleep and work in the top room, up in the eaves. It was wide and long with wooden floors, and a large skylight, so I'd be able to watch the stars at night. He asked for floor plans and measurements, and, later that night, sent by return three or four JPEGs of pages torn from his sketch pad. He'd drawn several plans in miniature, with sharp black lines delineating his vision for my writer's garret. He noted the extra pieces of furniture I'd need to buy, and the sort of desk he thought would work. He showed me where on the walls he would fix hooks, 'for your dresses'. Laughing, I printed the JPEGs and the emails, and stuck them in my notebook: 'By Robert, my American architect'.

That Friday at the new flat, I waited with Mike, my land-lord-to-be. Robert was slightly late and didn't smile. I stepped towards him to ask, was he OK, but Robert stuck out his hand.

'I'm Robert. You must be Elizabeth. We spoke on the phone. I'm so sorry I'm late, I was held up on a conference call.'

I looked at him, confused.

Then he shook Mike's hand. 'Robert. I'm the architect. Mind if I take a look upstairs? That's the room you'll have as your study, right, Elizabeth?'

I nodded, too stunned to speak. Mike said, 'Sure, go ahead,' then he smiled at me, raising both his eyebrows.

I shrugged, then I blushed, deeply.

Robert pulled a pad and a pencil from his bag, a tape measure from his pocket, and disappeared upstairs.

Mike said nothing about it, nor did I. We walked the rest of the apartment, running through windows and locks and spare keys and utilities providers. When we'd finished, I said, in passing, that Robert was a friend of a friend, and was doing me some sketches for free, just for fun. Neither of us referred to my rent reduction.

Robert jogged down the stairs, tucked his notebook in his pocket and said, 'I think that's everything. Good to meet you.' He shook hands with both of us, then he said to me with a half-smile, 'I'll be in touch,' and went.

When I left a little later, leaving Mike to lock up, I got a text from Robert telling me to meet him at a bar in Shoreditch.

'Are you crazy?' I said when I found him. 'What was that?'

'I thought that's what we were doing! You said, I could pretend –'

'I was joking. We were joking. It was a joke.'

'I know. So was I.'

'I didn't mean, pretend to Mike. I meant, pretend to each other. What does that look like? He's given me a rent reduction and I show up with my architect.'

'Relax. He won't think about it like that. Everyone has architects.'

'Everyone who?'

'Come on! It was fun.'

'For you, maybe. You know what, you're a very good liar.'

He would be in Oman the weekend I moved. He felt bad, he said, and asked if there was some other way he could help.

I joked that he might cancel his flight and skip his conference.

'Errr –'

'I'm kidding, Robert. Have a good trip. Come and see me when you're back.'

Mike had recommended a man with a van for the move, who charged by the hour. Magali and Olivier helped me with the smaller things, which we drove over in their car. When we were done, Olivier went to the club, and Magali and I took a bottle of wine to the attic room and cleaned the soot from the skylight. Opening it right back, we stood on my bed and hung half out, looking north-west. We drank our wine, and saw the sun set.

'Are you in love yet, or what?' she asked.

'I don't know.'

'Are you gonna be?'

'Maybe.'

Robert came back from Oman and offered to help dispose of the things I had no room for.

First, he contacted the council, who arranged to take some spare furniture, for a family without any. The rest, he said, I should sell.

'*Lena used this site when she was moving to Primrose Hill,*' he emailed. '*She said they were good for downsizing.*'

Opening the link, I found an eBay middleman for the wealthy. Items of clothing, for example, with a minimum value of £1,500, could be collected and sold on for a small commission.

'*How about you just come to my housewarming tea?*' I wrote back the next day, when he asked if the site had proved useful. '*Come and celebrate. Come and meet some more of my friends.*'

On the Sunday morning, I told him I was going to the supermarket. 'Before it gets busy. I have to come back and bake before three. People are coming at four.' He got his jacket. 'What're you doing?'

'I'm coming too.'

'What for?'

'I'll help.'

'Help with what?'

He reminded me that he'd accepted my invitation conditionally: he would come as co-host, rather than guest. 'Co-hosts get to go shopping, too.'

At the supermarket, he made suggestions, but was happy in the main to hold the baskets, and watch me tick my list, and listen to my plans to bake scones and cupcakes. Outside, I let him take the bags but said, 'What do I carry? What am I supposed to do?'

'Nothing. That's my job. I'm the guy. You just get to walk.'

My hands felt empty. My arms light, and slightly useless. I could see him sweating, just a tiny bit, and could see the bag handles straining. 'Let's get the bus. It might be quicker. It's not such nice weather for walking, anyway.'

The bus stop was next to a vintage dress shop. Looking in the window, Robert asked what I'd be wearing.

'What do you mean?'

'For your tea party. What'll you wear?'

'This!' I laughed, looking down at my jeans. 'What else? It's just tea. We're just hanging out.'

He took my arm and pulled me into the shop. 'Choose a dress. Any dress. Let me see you try them on.'

Straight away, he set down the bags and was pulling dresses from hangers and calling over the assistant and I was being led into the changing room and he was lifting aside the curtain to watch.

Each time I was ready, he let the curtain drop and I walked around the store.

There was one dress he liked more than any other.

'Why?' I asked. To me it was nondescript, or even bag-ish.

'I like your shape in it.'

'But you can't see my shape,' I said.

'I can see it when you move.' He came over and tied the tiny belt a little bit tighter, so it cinched at my waist. 'It's very, very sexy.'

Still I didn't get it, until the assistant handed me a necklace and a short-cut cardigan, and it made sense: I could see the kind of woman he wanted me to be.

On the bus, he held the bags, and slung the one from the dress shop over his chest. Hanging on to the passenger rail, I swung gently, looking at this man who had bought me a dress, and was travelling with the crowds on a lunchtime bus, because I'd said no to a cab.

Before anyone arrived, Robert hoovered the apartment. He said he had to, and how could I think of letting people see it in that state? He went back over the stair carpet again, then he asked if I'd spoken to my landlord about getting it replaced.

'The stairs just are that colour,' I said when he said he would make a third attempt. 'Why not leave it? No one who's coming will notice. Though, actually, maybe it's good for you. Is this your first time with a Hoover?'

I made cupcakes, and wore the new dress he'd bought me. I liked the unfamiliarity of the silk, and the way it felt against my skin.

In the afternoon, I invited my friends to sit at the table in the window, looking out at my new neighbourhood: there was a fruit and flower wholesaler, managed by a boy who looked to be no more than fourteen, and a launderette which had retained its 1950s sign.

Robert had aligned everything so perfectly, though, and pushed every chair in so tightly, it was impossible to pull one out. Everyone laughed, then they stood for a while looking at the fruit boy, while I rearranged the room.

In the photos he took of that day, I am wearing an apron over my new silk dress. On the work surface behind me there are yellow tulips in a vase, loose and tumbling. I'm holding a mixing bowl against my hip, and a wooden spoon, and the sun slants across me and some flour is rising from the bowl and I am laughing. My apron, with its small, pink flowers, sits against the pale green silk and my belly rises softly.

'Was it nice,' Olivier said at the club the next evening, 'to have someone to carry your bags?'

'It was strange. I didn't know what to do.'

'You'd rather do everything for yourself?' A series of images flashed through my mind: late nights back from the library, bike paniers full of books or groceries, balancing my bike while I unlocked the door. I didn't answer.

'It's just a strange idea. I'm well. I'm strong. I'm fit. I don't need anyone for that.'

'For other things?'

'I have friends if I need someone. If I'm ill I mean. If I fall off my bike. I can ask people. I can ask you and Magali.'

'Do you always want to ask?'

On the 14th, Robert took me for a Valentine's Day breakfast at Delaunay's.

The waitress recognised us from our first date, and asked us how we were.

In our response, we played the parts of a married couple, or a pair of long-term lovers. While he smiled at her and made small talk, I smiled with him. Half liking the lie, at the same time I half hated it, and wanted to say to her: we barely know each other; I will be surprised if, within a month, we are still together; I don't think I'll ever see you again.

'No bike helmet today?' she said to me, and I remembered having balanced it on the back of my chair on our first visit.

'Ah!' I said, gesturing to my green silk dress. 'Wrong gear for cycling!'

She left, and I reached into my bag and gave him my Valentine's gift: two tea-light holders cut from tin, with tiny holes punched in them, to form hearts for the lights to shine through.

He looked a little embarrassed, and gave me a pair of leather gloves in return: lined with fur, they were cut for a man and two sizes too big. They were wrapped in newspaper, and I remembered having seen them at his apartment once, when I'd looked in a cupboard to borrow a jumper.

Our food came. Almost straight away, before we took a mouthful, he asked me to go with him to Washington that afternoon.

'But I told you, when you asked yesterday. I can't. I'm working.'

'It's a week.'

'Exactly. A whole week's work.'

'We could have such a good time together.'

'I don't get it. You're going there for meetings. How would that be having a good time together?'

Still insisting, he laid out our itinerary. There were so many caveats and restrictions, he took some time explaining that in the mornings (while he worked) I could visit galleries and museums and bookstores, and for lunch (while he would be entertaining clients), I could try the museum cafes, or he could recommend brasseries. In the afternoons (while he would be on site visits), I could sightsee, or if I became bored of that, he said, I could enjoy the hotel spa, and relax in the room.

In the evenings, there were people I could meet ('She's an old college friend, totally relaxed') and people I couldn't ('They knew Lena, they're too conservative, they wouldn't get it'). At the end of the week, I'd fly back a day ahead of him: Philippe would be in town for a night and it was too soon to introduce us, he said.

When he was done, I looked at my watch and said he had spent almost an hour telling me what I could do on a trip I wasn't taking, instead of enjoying the time we were having.

'You're really not coming?'

'I'm not.'

'Because you're working?'

'Exactly.'

'You know what I think our problem is, Elizabeth?'

'Tell me.'

'We're at such different stages of our careers. I made partner last year.'

'So?'

'You're kinda starting out. You've had two, three novels out? I understand. You still have to establish yourself. I think that's why our work patterns are so opposed.'

'Opposed?'

'If you could just take a week off every now and again, I could take you places you've never been. Show you the world!'

'Take me on your work trips, you mean?'

'It's a free holiday for you. Give yourself a break sometimes, that's all I'm saying.'

'I don't need a break. I love my work. And I'm never going to work less hard. Even when I've − whatever you just called it, "established myself".'

'Never?'

'When I'm your age, I'll just be hitting my stride. That's when the really hard work will start.'

'Well, I don't know what to say.'

'I'm teasing, Robert. I told you already, I'm not coming with you to Washington. How can you act surprised?'

'I just feel like I'm doing all the running here.'

'It's your choice to go.'

'I have to work.'

'So do I. How exactly does that mean you're doing all the running?'

'You never call when I'm away. It's always me that calls.'

'Do you know what I'm charged for international, on my mobile?'

'Is that why? You never told me that.'

'I thought it was obvious.'

'Listen to me. Let's make a deal. If you call me, or message me or email me, I will call you right back. Any time. Whatever I'm doing. If I can't call at that exact moment, I'll say right away when I can. OK?'

'OK.'

'I promise,' he said. 'I will make myself permanently available.'

At his apartment, I watched him pack his case. He wanted me to admire the system he'd developed for his work trips: the order he placed things in, and the internal storage bags he used. Unpacking the case again, he demonstrated the ease with which, at the other end, he'd be able to find what he needed.

'I want to pack you too,' he smiled. 'I want to fold you up and make you tiny. I want to take you with me. Listen, honey. If you change your mind after I've gone, fly out. I'll email you a ticket. Just come.' He gave me a small card, with an address. 'This is where I'm staying. And if you want to use this place while I'm away, here's Mimi's number. She'll lend you her keys. When I'm back I'll get you a set.'

From Washington, he brought me a bracelet.

He'd found it on his last day, in a gallery Philippe had taken him to. It was a single piece of coiled black metal, which sat in a fat ring that could be stretched and slipped over my hand, then coiled tight and snug on my wrist. Philippe had found it, he said, in the gallery shop.

'Do you think he knew who you were buying it for?'

'Probably not.'

'You didn't say?'

'Nope.'

'He didn't ask?'

'Nope. I didn't ask about *his* love life, either. And he didn't tell. And I'm OK with that.'

He showed me photographs of the two of them together, standing in front of that museum.

'He's tall!' I said.

'It's because of Lena. I mean, the guy's three inches taller than me! It's amazing.'

'Boys always grow taller than their mothers.'

'She gave him that, for sure. I gave him his eyes.'

I looked more closely, and saw what he meant. 'They're like molasses.'

Robert laughed. 'You're right. I'm telling you, look at 'em. He must have girls going crazy for 'em. I know I did when I was his age. But I never had quite his height. That would've been something.'

'I still don't get why you can't tell him about us.'

'It's complicated. He's vulnerable.'

'So, he thinks you're a born-again virgin, now you and Lena are separated?'

'He thinks of me as his dad. That's the only way he knows me.'

'He's an adult. He knows you're an adult. What does he think you do for sex?'

'There's nothing really to tell him.'

'When *is* there going to be? What has to happen before you mention my existence? It just feels like you're hiding me.'

'Honey, we're not even, you know, living together.'

'I've only known you three months.'

'Exactly. So what's there to tell?'

'You leave enough things in my apartment. I'd say that's something to tell. Last week I counted forty-eight red socks. It's practically a pop song.'

'You counted?'

'They're everywhere. How many red socks do you own? Do you not have any in your own place any more? Is that the only reason you visit me, to get yourself some socks?'

More recently, an umbrella had appeared. Magali grabbed it from the coat rack one day, to run over to the fruit stall. Heavy and tall and bone-handled, its price tag was still attached.

'Who spends £80 on an umbrella then leaves it some-where?' Magali said. 'Who does that?'

'Oh, I think it was on purpose. I said the only things he ever leaves here are his socks.'

'And?'

'And that that showed a lack of commitment.'

'Ha!'

'Well, it does. I've left tons of actual stuff at his place. Stuff I'd mind if I never saw again. All I get is his socks.'

'Have you guys swapped keys yet?'

'Nope.'

'Have you asked him?'

'Nope.'

'Has he asked you?'

'Nope.'

'That's more important than leaving stuff. Keys is the next stage.'

A week or so later, he left his Brompton.

'He got himself another,' I explained to Magali.

'Another Brompton?'

'He said it was a good excuse. He wanted a different colour. He said if he gave it to me, he could justify the expense of getting himself a new one. The colour he's chosen has to be spray-painted, so he needs a plain frame.'

'I never knew you wanted a Brompton.'

'I don't.'

'Are you gonna use it?'

'I can't. I tried, but the handlebar is too low.'

'Can't you just raise it?'

'A bit, but it's pretty much fixed. With Bromptons you choose the bits you want and put them together. He has a longer back than me. A different body. This one fits his body but it doesn't fit mine.'

'Did you tell him?'

'Yes.'

'But he still left it here?'

'He said he'd customise it for me.'

'How?'

'He's got a whole workshop. A lock-up, you know, for bike stuff, at the back of his apartment block He said he'd do it with an angle grinder.'

'He has an angle grinder?'

'He practically made his last racer from scratch.'

'Don't go hanging about in a workshop with a guy wielding an angle grinder.'

'I probably won't. He said I can just sell the whole thing on eBay and use the cash to buy another model.'

'A different Brompton?'

'Yes.'

'Would you want another Brompton, though? That's what I still don't get.'

'No.'

'So are you gonna sell it on eBay?'

'I don't think he really meant for any of that to happen. I think he just wanted to leave it here. It's like dogs, you know, and lamp posts.'

That weekend, at a restaurant in Exmouth Market, he pulled something from his pocket.

'Close your eyes and open your hands.'

When I looked again, I was holding four rubber key caps. He was smiling.

'There you go, honey.' Reaching into his bag for a set of keys, he fitted the caps and talked me through his colour code.

When he was done, he asked for a set of mine. 'They'll cut them at the hardware store. It's right around the corner. I could drop them in while you order coffee.'

'I need to think about it.'

'Is that your way of saying you're not giving me your keys?'

'No. It's my way of saying I need to think about it. Want to come by Magali's club later?'

'Who's playing.'

'An amazing trio.'

'Jazz?'

'Of course. It's a jazz club, you know it is.'

'I mean, I'm just not so into jazz.'

'That doesn't matter. It's just a nice place to hang out. They'll keep us a table if we're there by eight. You can meet some more of my friends.'

'I don't think so. You can't really talk, with music.'

'You don't want to meet them?'

'I do. Let's invite them over, though. Have a conversation.'

That week at my new place, we had a dinner party for my friends.

Again he insisted on co-hosting, and kept my apron on until the last moment, so he was still wearing it when the first people came.

He was easy at first, and found common ground with everyone. Through the evening, though, he talked more and more about his life with Lena. ('We have a house in Connecticut,' or, 'When our boy was small, we went to Maine every summer. Lena's mom has a place there, and a boat,' and, 'We have chickens in our garden in London.') At first, I thought it was only me who was made uncomfortable, but when the chickens were spoken of, as though he and Lena still shared a home, I noticed glances being exchanged, and raised eyebrows. Once, I caught my friend's eye and raised my eyebrows back, but I waited until the last person left.

'How can you say you love me and say "we" all night?'

'What?'

'"We have chickens at our house at Hampstead"? Do you realise it sounded as though you're still with her?'

'No, honey.'

'Yes, honey. "We have chickens at our house." That was embarrassing! Nothing you said sounded like you'd left her. It was as though I invited both of you but she cancelled last minute, so you came on your own. You're not ready for this, are you?'

He knelt in front of me and closed his eyes. He wrapped his arms around my legs and pressed his face into my thighs.

'But I am. Lena and I aren't together any more.'

I stroked his head. He shook once, twice, as though he was crying. It was some time before he pulled back.

'What does this look like, Robert?' I said, thinking that he might be about to acknowledge that he wasn't ready to commit to someone new. 'The two of us sitting here crying?'

'I don't know.'

'It looks to me like this isn't working out.'

'You're wrong.'

'What, then?'

'It looks to me like I need you, and it looks like you need me. We were good together tonight. It's just syntax, that "we" stuff. It's just you and me now.'

The morning after, we cleared up from the dinner.

'How do you feel about the smell in this place?' he asked.

'What smell?'

'You are kidding. The kebab shop downstairs. That fan is going the whole day.'

'Oh. I don't mind it. It's not a kebab shop. It's a Turkish restaurant. I like the guys there. They're friendly. When I come back late, they look out for me. You should talk to them.'

'Do you?'

'Course. I walk past them every time I come home. Sometimes they call me in for tea and ask me how my day was. And their hummus is to die for.'

'My shirts smell. I go to work smelling like a kebab.'

'So leave your shirts at work. Change when you get there.'

'I don't think that'll fix it. It's on my skin, you know? In my hair.'

'So don't stay over.'

'I like staying over.'

'So don't complain.'

He agreed with me about the neighbourhood. The flowers and the fruit and the launderette were attractive, he said, and interesting to watch from the window. It was convenient to have a bus stop just outside, and the Tube round the corner. He said he thought he could get used to the place, in time.

He drew a line, though, when I found a flatmate to help with the rent.

'We'll have to just stay at mine from now on. I'm sorry.'

'Hey, he's a perfectly nice guy. I thought you got on when you met.'

'We did. But I'm fifty-two. I just can't – I can't wait in line for the bathroom.'

'Well, have a conversation. Figure it out. Talk to him about what time you need to leave in the morning. It's what people do!'

'What people?'

'People who flat-share.'

'He's at the Cass, for Chrissake. He's a student in the school of architecture I'm a guest speaker at every month.'

'Fine,' I said. 'Do what you like. This is my life. No one told you to be my boyfriend.'

He kept coming back. My new flatmate had a girlfriend south of the river, and was often there. When he was at home, he got up later than Robert in any case, so they rarely overlapped.

In that attic room where I slept and wrote the wind came through the roof tiles. It was cold, so I used two heaters when I worked. At 5 a.m., I was woken by the buses on the Bethnal Green Road. First there was the roar, when it was still some way away, then there was a rumble.

'My bed moves,' I said to him once when it had woken me, and I had woken him. 'Do you mind?'

'It's not ideal,' he agreed.

'I can't believe my bed actually moves because of a bus.'

'It doesn't, not exactly. Probably what happens is that the passing bus is vibrating the road a tiny bit, which in turn passes some energy to your foundations and ultimately to the floor of your room. It's called resonance. If the original vibration is at just the right frequency, and if the floor just happens to be flexible enough, then this floor diaphragm magnifies the tiny oscillations into bigger waves, which in turn move your bed and all loose bits on your desk. You hear that?' he asked, as my pencil sharpener lifted and landed on my desk, then lifted and landed again.

Next time he emailed, he attached a short movie clip of the Tacoma Narrows Bridge collapsing, with a note:

It's not strictly resonance that you see here. Actually it's aero-elastic flutter. They tried so hard to tie this one down, honey. Stays, extra girdle cables, every last thing. It was never going to hold. Too narrow for the length. Shaky from day #1 and got shakier.

In the clip, a screen title flashes up: 'DISASTER'. The trees are tossed in a high wind and the bridge flips and twists like rubber. There are passers-by, strolling rather than hurrying, then another screen title, 'THE CRASH', and the camera is on the bridge looking at a lone car. A man gets out of the car and moves towards the camera. Another man appears, wearing a mackintosh and cupping a pipe. His hair rises in the wind and he casts only one glance over his shoulder before the camera angle pulls back and the bridge heaves and flips and is breaking into pieces.

I wrote to Robert about that clip, and mentioned the man in the mackintosh, cupping his pipe. Robert wrote back that he was a Professor Farquharson, who five days earlier had come up with a solution to stabilise the bridge. There wasn't time to try it, and in the seconds before the bridge collapsed into the Puget Sound, the professor returned to the bridge to try to rescue a dog from the abandoned car, left there by its driver, a Mr Coatsworth, who had failed to persuade it to go with him. The dog, Robert wrote, was still too terrified to leave the vehicle, and bit the professor's hand.

What about this? For the car, the Coatsworth guy got a hundred bucks more than he did for the dog! He was taking that dog back to his daughter. $364.40? That dog might've been everything to our Mr Coatsworth's daughter. $364.40. She might have loved that dog more than she loved her own father.

When the winter storms came, I woke sometimes and heard the wind. Listening to my pencils, lifting and falling on the desk, I would picture Mr Coatsworth's dog biting the hand of its would-be rescuer. The fall wasn't shown in the clip but I thought of it so much I came to imagine that I'd seen it. I would wake up sometimes, hearing the slap of skin and fur on the ice-cold water.

He gave me what he called 'cold-weather gifts': a small cashmere cardigan, and several pairs of thick woollen socks.

'You shouldn't have.'

'It's nice. It's nice for me and it's nice for you.'

In return, I bought him things for his apartment. All of them were small, and inconsequential, but one of them was expensive, so I had it delivered to his office, instead of the communal hallway of my flat at Bethnal Green. When he brought it back already opened, I expressed surprise and he said, 'Why wouldn't I open it? It was addressed to me.'

'To me. *Care of* you.'

'It came to my office.'

'But it was supposed to be a surprise! I was supposed to wrap it up and give you it.'

'This is a present? For me?'

Inside was a small, rectangular piece of wood. Painted to look like the cover of a book, it had holes drilled into its spine and two screws for attaching it, horizontally, to the wall. The title of the book was painted in bold black letters: *Ceci n'est pas un livre*. Piled on top of this, a stack of books would appear to be floating on the wall, the pretend-bookshelf rendered invisible.

It made him smile, but instead of fixing it up and stacking real books on top of it, he put it on a bookshelf among his other books and left it there. I mentioned it once or twice, but he changed the subject. I did think about asking for it back, to give it to someone else who might have used it. The way he'd responded to my giving him it, though, suggested I shouldn't.

Apart from the bracelet from Washington, all of Robert's gifts to me were practical. Usually he chose things he knew I needed, so that I unwrapped them and used them straight away. There were some bike lights, for example, which he had owned for just a few months and was discarding in favour of newer, sleeker versions. The ones on my bike were less visible than they should have been, so I thanked him and clipped them on to cycle home that evening.

In return for the bike lights, I gave him a novel.

When he unwrapped the slender blue-and-white hard-back, he seemed nonplussed. I told him it had been shortlisted for the Pulitzer, and I offered to read him the first chapter. He said, half-heartedly, 'OK. I guess. Maybe later,' then he showed me the cover.

'*Train Dreams.* You're giving me a book about trains?'

'Actually, no. It's about a guy. A guy called Robert.'

'That's why?'

'Actually, I chose it for the bridges. After you sent me the clip of the Tacoma Narrows Bridge, I remembered this novel. There are bridges in it. It's your kind of book. I think you'll like it.'

Later, after dinner, he lay back on the sofa with his eyes closed while I read aloud.

When I got to the part where Grainier caught the Chinaman-suspect's feet tighter and exclaimed, 'I've got the bastard!' Robert's eyes opened. Throughout the fugitive's desperate escape over the side of the half-completed railway bridge, fifty feet above the Moyea River, Robert's eyes flicked back and forth. When the Chinaman screamed out his curse and vanished, he shut his eyes tight, but I glanced over once or twice and saw they were moving, underneath his eyelids. As Grainier walked home that night, imagining he could see the Chinaman everywhere, Robert's eyes flicked back and forth rapidly, as though he was there too, watching the woods and the road and the creek.

In the months to come, before our love affair ended, he would read and reread this book, slowly and carefully. I would find him in the bedroom sometimes, falling asleep with it resting on his stomach. In the mornings, if I got up before him and came back to bed with coffee, he'd be buried in its pages and hardly notice me.

He said nothing at all to me about it, and though he was always reading it, never seemed close to finishing. It was only after we split that he spoke about it, on the phone once, when he said he was reading it a third time, and was glad I'd given him it.

March

How to tell if the moon is waxing or waning

If a crescent moon hangs in the shape of a 'C', for the word 'crescendo', it is waning.

If it is the opposite, and forms the curve of a capital 'D', which we might think of as the start of the word 'decrescendo', the moon is, in fact, waxing.

So we can remember the rule like this: the moon always lies.

Cedric Chester, *A Moon-spotter's Almanac*

For the club's first birthday, Magali and Olivier booked a trio from New York.

'You're kidding,' I said when she told me who. 'How?'

'I called up their agent and I hustled. They're playing Ronnie's the next two Thursdays so they're over here anyway. I want to make some noise. Shout about it. We're celebrating.'

By the time I arrived, she'd sent out for more champagne, twice, and crates of Havana Club Gran Reserva, which her father had ordered for everyone.

'Limes,' Olivier said, passing Magali the phone. 'We need more limes.'

'Are you warm enough?' she asked me. I nodded, and took off my jacket. 'Heating's fixed,' she smiled. 'I think that's made me happier than anything. Limes.' She headed for the office. 'I'm going to call a guy about limes.'

I was at the bar when Robert arrived. He'd told me he would bring someone, and when I saw her first of all I thought I knew her. 'Why didn't you tell me,' I whispered to him while her coat was checked, 'you were bringing a celeb?'

'Hardly.'

'Well, she is, you know, *known*. I'm so sorry but I can't actually remember her name.'

'Exactly.'

'Please tell me. I'm too embarrassed to ask.'

'She's called Juliet. She's well known, honey, but she's not a celeb. You'll get to meet her properly next week.'

'I will?'

'Wednesday evening? You said you'd come. I hope it's OK to have brought her tonight. I'd forgotten I'd told her we'd go for drinks, just the two of us. Didn't want to let you down, so I just asked Juliet along.'

'Of course. The more the merrier. Rum?' I suggested, as a tray of cocktails went past.

'No thanks.' Then the well-known actor came back and she and Robert were absorbed. I walked the room, embracing my friends, and Magali's and Olivier's. I looked over at Robert, thinking I should be taking him around with me, introducing him. Then I realised it was better this way. I liked being ostensibly single. It was how I'd always related to the people who were there that night, and with each embrace I hoped that Robert and Juliet would remain engrossed.

When they found me, an hour or more on, I'd had too much rum to be able to have the kind of conversation Robert wanted.

'What about a drink?' I said to him.

'You have one already, honey.'

'Juliet doesn't,' I smiled. 'Do you like cocktails, Juliet?'

'I do, as a matter of fact.'

'There you are, see? Go to the bar and get your friend a cocktail, Robert. Or she'll feel awfully left out. I can personally recommend the Po-littles, Juliet. Really gorgeous.'

'Po-littles?'

'Oops. Li-tans. Cosmo-po-li-tans. Robert, get me one too, will you?'

In Robert's absence, Juliet and I had very little to say to one another. The musicians were taking a break, and the fill-in records were too loud for chatting in any case. Robert arrived with the cocktails and the musicians returned to the stage. In the second's silence before they started up, Juliet whispered to Robert that she wasn't sure, but was that an ant in her cocktail? Or two, maybe?

'Oh, you lucky thing,' I whispered. 'Here, let's swap. D'you mind? I love ants. They're my absolute favourite.'

At 1 a.m., Robert kindly, sweetly, gently, helped me into a cab.

'Where's the well-known lady actor?' I said. 'Isn't she coming home with us?'

'She left two hours ago, honey. When you were hugging the small number of guys in the room who hadn't already hugged you.'

In the morning, I found it hard to sit up.

'There was nothing nice about it, that's all I'm saying.'

I opened my eyes. Then I opened my mouth to answer but my eyes hurt, and my head hurt. Sitting up for a second, I saw the room move, so I closed my eyes again and lay back down. I wanted to speak, but my lips were too dry, and when I tried, my tongue stuck to them.

Robert carried on. 'I just don't see how you can expect me to think of you as a maternal person.'

'Hmm?' I could say that without opening my mouth, or my eyes. I said it again, a little louder. 'Hmmm?'

'It's not the kind of behaviour I'd expect from someone who wants to be a mother, that's what I mean. Do you have any idea what being a parent would actually involve?'

'Please,' I whispered. 'Please could I have some water? A really large, really cold glass of water?'

When he'd gone for the water, I stood up. Sitting down again, I tried to work out how close I was to vomiting, and what I'd do it in if I did. I opened the skylight, but the sun was too bright to keep my head out for long, and the height made me dizzy. I took a sip of water from a bottle on my desk, and practised saying a word, then a whole sentence. When he came up again, I was in bed, under the sheet.

'I've got to leave, Elizabeth. I'm going to be late for work.'

'OK, babe,' I said. 'Thanks for coming. It was so –'

I heard him dressing. When I opened my eyes, he'd gone.

In the afternoon he emailed, and asked if he could come to dinner at my place.

He arrived, and I apologised.

'It's OK.' The flowers he gave me were tall white roses and purple irises. 'Let's not talk about it. Are you OK? Are you –?'

'Hung-over? Yes, of course I am. So will everyone be. Apart from you. I imagine even Juliet might have a small headache.'

'It's OK. I know, I overreacted. I've never seen you like that before, that's all.'

'Of course you haven't. I hardly ever get "like that". I should tell you that most of the people there last night happen to be parents. And pretty much all of them had more to drink than I did. It was a celebration, Robert. A big deal. Do you know how hard it is to open a club in London and make it work for a year? They've done brilliantly. Everyone wanted to have a good time.'

'OK. I said, I know, I overreacted. Do you like your flowers?'

'I love them.'

After dinner, he worked on a talk he was due to give in Frankfurt. Every now and again I put down the book I was reading, and made a note in my journal. Later, when he asked about the journal, I showed him a few of the pages. There were poems I'd liked and copied out, and sometimes a photograph Sellotaped in. Once or twice, I'd stapled in a ticket or a programme, to remind me of a show. On another of the pages was a pencil sketch of Highbury Fields, which I'd cycled past one evening. The sky to the west had fallen that night into a broad purple band which sat on the roofs of the houses. The crescent moon was high above this band, in a part of the sky which had remained a pale grey-blue. I had drawn the roofs and the sky and the trees as childishly geometric shapes, and the moon as a single curved line. Beneath my sketch I had written: '*The new moon is a baby's fingernail, thrown into the sky.*'

He studied the words, then he asked me to describe the scene as though I was telling a story. 'Wait, wait a second.' He took his artist's sketchbook from his pocket and flipped it open. As I began to speak, with his pocket watercolours and working fast, he recreated what I'd seen. I said the final word, and he tore the page from his sketchbook and, before the paint had dried, made me a present of it. It was my sketch but in colour, and with perspective: he had made it real.

'Might not have been a new moon, though,' he said.

'Hmmm?'

'Which way was the crescent facing?'

'I can't remember.'

'Know how to tell if a moon is new or old?'

'No,' I said. 'It just looked new!'

'It might have been dying, not newborn. Let me tell you how.'

He suggested we spend the following Saturday walking the Regent's Canal from King's Cross to Limehouse. On the Friday, I bought a new coat. For the first time in my life, I chose one that wasn't blue or black, but instead, dark red. It was cut close to my body, with sleeves that were ruched on the shoulder. For our walk, I wore it with a black cloche hat and black gloves, which my brother had given me for Christmas. I tied Robert's black crêpe scarf high on my neck.

We met by a bridge, at exactly the point where the path comes up at Granary Square. The sky was bright, and the air cold. He wore a thick wool jacket and a brown felt trilby, and we stood in an embrace for some time, our two hats together.

When he let me go I showed him the patterns on the water. He took my hand and moved it, so that I pointed instead to where the shaft of sun was playing onto the underside of the bridge, flung back from the canal, then he explained the angle of incidence. We sat on the steps for some time in silence, holding hands and watching passers-by. In the square we saw the fountains. He took photographs and made me laugh, pushing me away and pulling me into him.

We walked for hours that day, our words falling over one another and our hands entwined.

That evening I emailed Susie, who had written to ask how my writing was going, and how things were with Robert, who she hadn't seen at book group for a while.

'*Don't worry!*' I wrote. '*He's alive and well; I haven't done away with him. I haven't been writing, or not enough, but he has made me smile again. Really smile, I mean. I think my face had forgotten what it felt like. My cheeks hurt from smiling.*'

Looking at the photos of that day I see myself clasped to his chest while he holds the camera out. When he held me like that, right in close with my head leaning into him, my cloche hat was tucked just under the brim of his trilby. He had been playful, so that some of the pictures are of just the tops of our faces, or of just the bottom half. In one picture, at his suggestion, our eyes are shut tight on purpose and we are smiling.

In the last two, I am sitting on a stone bench in the square, half turned away from him. There are clutches of small children playing by the fountains, just to the right of me. My gaze is trained on them.

I thought that's what he was seeing too, when he took those pictures.

I thought that's why he was taking them.

The children had been laughing and running into and out of the jets of water. One of them, a girl of perhaps four or five, had run past me and brushed against my knee and I was close enough to have reached out and caught her in my arms and picked her up and held her.

When I turned and saw that he was taking a picture of me and the children, I felt quite sure that we would be a family, and that we would bring our children to the square one day and watch them play in the water.

He stayed over at my apartment that night, before going straight to the Middle East.

I set my alarm for 5 a.m. to make him breakfast, ahead of his early Tube to Heathrow.

He looked surprised when I woke him to say it was ready, but he padded downstairs and ate with me.

Afterwards, he took my hand, to lead me back upstairs. 'Shall we?'

'Don't you have to pack?'

'We have an hour, honey. More.' He slipped his hand between my thighs.

'It's just after six.'

'Even better. So we have nearly two hours.'

'You're kidding. Why are we awake, then? Why aren't we sleeping?'

It was a misunderstanding, he said. His flight had been changed and he'd forgotten to tell me.

'That's not a misunderstanding, Robert. That's you not thinking of telling me. That's different.'

But he was pulling at his pyjamas, and taking my hand to feel how stiff he was. 'This way we get longer for sex.'

I pushed him away. I said it was an ordinary day for me. I'd made my plans around his early departure, and I had a new chapter to start. I'd use my extra hour on that, and would be grateful if he could pack and leave.

'Are you serious, Elizabeth?'

'When you go to work in London, on an ordinary day, you leave first thing, right?'

'Of course.'

'You never linger.'

'Right.'

'Even if I asked you to, you wouldn't, would you?'

'But it's different for me,' he protested. 'There are other people involved. I have meetings.'

'And I have characters, waiting for me to tell them what to do. I have a contract for a book I haven't written yet.'

'Come on, honey. I'm leaving soon. I won't see you for a week. Your characters can wait an hour, can't they?'

I half let him pull me upstairs, then I stopped.

'I can't keep changing things to suit your work. You have to go. The only difference between my "other people" and your "other people" is that I have to make mine up. Every thought they think, every word they speak, and every single thing they do. You're lucky, Robert. You pack your case, get on a plane, and when you get off at the other end, your "people" are waiting in arrivals, holding up a little sign with your name on. I'll be home from the library by about seven. If you miss me too much, fly back from Doha. Drop your "other people" like you're asking me to drop mine.'

He went to take a shower. Later, I heard the front door, and realised he'd gone without saying goodbye.

I phoned him, but he didn't take my call.

That night, I emailed.

I wrote that when I'd asked him to leave, what I'd really wanted to say was, stay. I wished he was still there. I missed him, I was sorry to have been bad-tempered, and please would he remind me about the angle of incidence, from our canal walk? I'd been thinking of what he'd told me, and couldn't quite remember.

In the morning, I was woken by the rain on my skylight.

When it stopped, a seagull landed and stood on the glass, shaking the drops from its back. I watched, then my alarm went off and the seagull looked down at me. I stood up on the bed, my sheet pulled around me, and put my hand to where the bird was. It flew away, and the sky cleared.

Robert had replied overnight.

Angle of incidence measures inclination relative to an established reference. A more useful bit of information: in optics, the angle of incidence always equals the angle of refraction. A ray of light will 'bounce' off a reflective surface at the same angle that it arrived. The angle of incidence is usually measured relative to 'normal', an imaginary line that is perpendicular to the reflective surface. Sometimes the inclination is measured relative to the surface of the water; this is known as the glancing angle. The phenomenon accurately predicts all sorts of things, like the inflected path of a perfectly smooth marble ricocheting off a polished stone somewhere in the vacuum of outer space. Or perhaps the trajectory of an overly ardent suitor after confronting the brittle object of his attention.

I wrote back, that something was changing, with that brittleness, and that I didn't want him to feel like a man refracted. Then I told him about my storm-blown bird and he replied right away.

I know you didn't want me to go but I have to go sometimes.
That's what I do. That's what I'll always do. I sometimes feel
like your stormed-up, sleepy bird, you know? Standing on glass,
looking down at the beautiful girl.

He sent a postcard.

On its face was a photograph of a family of lions. The shot was a close-up: the adult male reclining with the female and three cubs in a kind of embrace, so that he lay half over them and the arm of one of the cubs was flung over its siblings. Apart from my name and address, in Robert's careful capitals, the back of the card was wordless. In the space left for a message, he'd drawn the outline of the adult female with his black felt tip. Her hollow head was inclined towards her cubs, her eye a crescent dash, shut fast in sleep.

The following week he took me to a supper party given by an opera director. Among the other guests was a cousin of Robert's who was a musician, and Juliet, who came on her own, just as she had for Magali's and Olivier's party. More musicians arrived later, after curtain-down, and one of the company asked him if he would like to finance their next show, in Vienna.

'Of course,' he said, smiling. 'Pitch it to me right now.'

I stayed for a while, and joined in with a few conversations until, suddenly, it seemed as though everyone was pretending to be someone they weren't. I didn't want to be there, and I left before him.

I went back to his place and texted to say sorry I'd left, and that I was tired. I'd go straight to bed, and he should come back anytime he liked: I'd be fast asleep so he wouldn't wake me.

Over breakfast, he told me about the rest of the party, and reported that the talk had turned to me. First, he said, was the opera director's description of my 'ferocious intelligence', which Robert said wasn't patronising. 'He was being nice, honey. He liked you!'

Then followed Juliet's views on my last novel. She told the party she'd discussed it with a 'close friend' who had sat on a prize panel which had, that year, rejected it.

'And then? What else am I to answer for?'

'There was one other topic.'

'Really? There was anything left to dissect, after all that?'

'What we are to one another.'

'And?'

'Juliet said it was for you to walk away.'

'I'm sorry?'

'If you want children. That's what she was referring to. She told me, "Robert, darling. It's not for you to tell her to leave. She must make up her own mind about that."'

'But *you* haven't made up *your* mind. You told me you were open to it, and that if you decided you weren't, you'd absolutely tell me straight away. That was our deal.'

'I did. And I will. That absolutely still applies. I'm just reporting what she said after you'd gone. Full disclosure.'

'Even if I was interested in what someone who's met me precisely twice, and barely so much as spoken to me on either occasion, has to say about my reproductive options, how could she possibly have formed an opinion about it being for me to walk away, unless *you'd* told her you didn't want kids? How?'

'Easy, honey, easy. Our deal stands. Can we look at flights for Vienna? They want us to be there for the opening. It would mean a lot to me if you'd come.'

Leaving his apartment after breakfast, I couldn't undo my bike lock. I tried for twenty minutes, by which time the backs of both my hands were grazed. Then I saw that the bike next to mine had been locked in such a way that, unless that other lock was removed, releasing my own was a physical impossibility.

I phoned Robert, up in his apartment.

'Where are you calling from?'

'Outside.'

'But you left a heap of time ago. What's happening?'

When he came down, I was crying with frustration.

'Honey, it's no big deal. We'll fix it.'

'It's not fixable.'

He moved my lock back and forth, then the other bike's. 'That's amazing,' he said, shaking his head. 'Who would do that? I'm apologising on behalf of my neighbour. It's so dumb, it's embarrassing.'

'Do you know whose it is?'

'I think so.'

'Can we call them?'

'Oh, he'll have gone already, for sure. He's never here during the day. Can you walk, just this time? We can knock him up tonight and ask him to move it.'

'No I can't. I'll be late for my brother. I told him to be early, so we'd have longer. He's hardly ever free for lunch. I've got to go back and change and get my stuff for the library this afternoon, send a bunch of emails then cycle to the City. I can't walk.'

'Listen. There's nothing to cry about. I'll call the guy, I'll find a way to fix it. I promise.'

He was away for five minutes, then he reappeared with a black case, made of hard rubber.

'What is that?'

'Don't worry, I've cleared this with him, he was already at his office. If you're gonna cycle today, it's our only option.'

He wore a transparent mask, and elbow-length work gloves. He shouted over the noise of the angle grinder, 'Stand back. No, further back!'

It was over so fast, I didn't have time to tell him it was unnecessary. That I could phone Will and explain, and ask him to reschedule.

Picking up the pieces of the neighbour's lock where they'd fallen, I asked Robert what he was planning to do with the bike.

'I'll keep it inside.' He pulled the mask from his face. 'I've told him to come pick it up tonight, and not be such a dumbass next time. Go, honey. I don't want you to be late.'

'But you saved me. You actually saved me.'

He took off his gloves, and put the grinder in its case. He kissed me, then he wiped my tears with his shirtsleeve. He wheeled my bike around and pointed it down the street. I sat on it, and he stepped forward, slipping his hands in his chino pockets and jogging just ahead of me, like a coach.

'C'mon, babe. You gotta go. I gotta go.' He turned back and smiled, with the sun on his molasses-brown eyes.

I cycled past him, laughing and calling, 'You look like Keanu Reeves. Did I ever tell you that? You look like a movie star.'

'No you didn't, and no I don't. Cycle safe, honey. Cycle safe and come back soon.'

Later, over lunch with my brother, I told him about Robert's deal, and about what the well-known actor had said.

'Doesn't matter what she said. It's simple. A fifty-two-year-old guy whose wife has left him is never going to turn down no-strings-attached sex with an attractive, intelligent, much younger woman. End of. So while he's "making his mind up", if that's what he wants to call it, how about freezing your eggs until you meet someone better?'

'I'm sorry?'

'He's unlikely to want any more kids. If he did, he wouldn't be keeping you waiting, would he? He'd be getting on with it. And so should you be.'

'But he's who I'm *with*. I haven't met anyone else.'

'What do you mean, you haven't met anyone else? Have you tried online?'

'Give me a break. What about your friends? Don't you know any handsome fertile bankers in need of a girlfriend?'

'Actually, now you mention it, you should meet –' and his phone was out of his pocket. 'No. On second thoughts, he's a prick. Sorry.' He put it away again.

'Thing is, I think I'm falling in love.'

'Think?'

'Know. I know I am. I love him.'

'That's delightful, Liz-bee. But I'm not kidding. You're forty. Why not freeze a few? This guy sounds like he's onto too much of a good thing to let you go, but nor is he going to do the decent thing and rule it out. He knows damn well that if he tells you he doesn't want kids, you'll be out of there. No more midnight sushi parties, no more showing you off to his geriatric friends, no more licky-sucky sleepovers.'

'Will!'

'Will, nothing. Don't say I didn't warn you. Take out a loan if you can't afford it. Why wouldn't you want to have kids? You'd be an amazing mum.'

Robert told me his son had a spring break coming up. For two weeks, Philippe would stay with his mother at her flat in Primrose Hill. Robert wanted to block out the dates, and keep them free, he told me, just in case.

'Have you guys made plans?'

'Oh, no. He's kind of a free spirit. He might want a night here, at my apartment. I told him he could sleep on the mezzanine. Dial out for pizza, watch Netflix.' He smiled. 'Bring girls. Eat sushi.'

'OK. Would you like to come to the BFI with me on Thursday? There's a special screening of *Truly Madly Deeply*. I love that movie.'

'Honey, I'd just rather keep things open.'

'Or the Complicite thing at the Barbican? They still had tickets when I looked.'

'You go ahead. I just want to be available for him. Totally, completely, available. It's only two weeks. It's not that I don't want to see you, I just – Pretend I'm on a trip, or something.'

'OK.'

'Don't be mad at me.'

'I'm not. I just didn't realise you had to be free for the whole two weeks. Even though you haven't actually got an actual plan to see him.'

'I'm sorry. It's just the way it is.'

'It's fine. It's wonderful you can clear your diary, just like that.'

I went back to Robert's place that afternoon, before he got home from work. When I'd collected the things I'd need for that fortnight, I stopped for a glass of water. The kitchen cupboards had been cleared of my food, and filled with taco shells, ketchup and Snickers bars. In the fridge, instead of yogurt and carrots and sparkling water, there were energy drinks, Coca-Cola, and three brands of beer.

A few days into Philippe's visit, Robert called. I was writing, with my phone on silent. When I surfaced, to get ready for the theatre, there were thirteen missed calls.

'What's the matter?' I said when he picked up. 'Are you OK?'

'I'm fine. What do you mean?'

'I missed your calls. I'm sorry, I was working.'

'Oh, it's no problem, I was just calling to ask if you wanted dinner tonight.'

'You called me thirteen times.'

'You didn't pick up.'

'Thirteen times? Just to ask me for dinner? I thought something awful had happened.'

'I wanted to hear your voice. I miss you.'

'OK.'

'OK? Is that all? Don't you miss me too?'

'Actually I was writing. I hadn't —'

'It's OK. You were working. So where do you want to go for dinner? Anywhere. Name your place.'

'I'm not free tonight. I'm seeing some Chekhov.'

'Can I come?'

'It's sold out. Hang on, I thought you were having Philippe over? Isn't he staying with you?'

'His mom's taking him to a bunch of things this week.'

'I've got to hang up now. I'm almost late.'

'You're going, just like that?'

'I said, I'm late. They're not going to hold the play because I got a call from my boyfriend.'

The same thing happened the next day, though it was fourteen times, not thirteen. We spoke briefly, and again I said I was rushing out, and would call another time. When he left ten messages on the Friday, I didn't call back. Coming home from a party in the early hours, my phone rang and I picked up straight away, thinking it was someone checking to see I was back OK.

'Wassup?' I said.

'Elizabeth? Are you OK?'

'Robert?'

'Honey, are you OK?'

'It's two in the morning. Why are you calling me? And yes, of course I'm OK. Why wouldn't I be?'

'You just slurred your words. You sound a little –'

'No, I didn't.'

'You said "wassup?"'

'That's a word, Robert.'

'What kind of a word?'

'It's a colloquial greeting favoured by young people. It's short for "what's up?" Which means "hello-how-are-you-what-can-I-do-for-you?" Anyway, please explain, why are you calling me at two in the morning?'

'I couldn't get a hold of you yesterday. I just wanted to see how you're doing, whether you wanna take a walk Sunday. Get brunch somewhere, see an exhibition?'

'We said we'd meet *next* weekend, when Philippe's gone. Saturday brunch, you said. And I'm walking home right now, in the dark, so I'd rather not be talking on the phone, if you don't mind. Why are you awake anyway? You never stay up this late.'

'I can't sleep. I miss you.'

'I'm going, honey. Call Philippe tomorrow, see if he's got any free time.'

'He doesn't pick up.'

'I'm sure he'll be in touch. He must just be busy, catching up with friends. He's been away a while, hasn't he?'

'OK.' His voice had switched to a flat, cold hardness. 'If that's the way you want it. Goodnight, Elizabeth,' and the line went dead.

I didn't hear from him at all that second week, so I emailed him on the Friday morning.

Dear Robert,
How are things? I hope you had some time with Philippe, and all's well.
Are you still free for brunch tomorrow? It's been a while! Meet at the cafe in Shoreditch, the one with the eggs you liked that time?
Elizabeth xx

He replied so late I'd begun to think he was freezing me out.

Dear Elizabeth,
I'd prefer to come over to your place. I'll be with you at 11.
R

I was annoyed, and wrote straight back.

Got cabin fever. Been writing all day and will carry on tonight, till late. I'd rather the cafe. If you don't want that, fine, we can meet another time.
E x

Almost before I hit 'send', there was his reply.

Sure. I'll reserve us a table for 11. Don't be tardy.
R

He opened with the accusation I'd expected.

'You're just not really into me, Elizabeth. You carry on with your life as though I don't exist. These last ten days –'

'These last ten days that were exactly what you asked for! Did you even think about how that would feel for me, being dropped for two weeks, because your son was in town? Did you consider introducing the two of us? Or what – am I some kind of guilty secret?'

'Philippe doesn't know about you yet. I can't just spring you on him.'

'If you don't even tell him you have a girlfriend, how will it ever not be "springing" me on him? And what would be so terrible about that anyway?'

'You don't understand. It would be massively significant for him. It would be like, I don't know –'

'Like what?'

'OK, here's what. It would be like some ultra-conservative guy telling his even more ultra-conservative father he's gay. Or something.'

'What the fuck?'

'I'm Philippe's dad. I'm married to Philippe's mom, you know.'

'You broke up! Or are you going back to her? Are the two of you talking things over?'

'That's not what I mean.'

'Well, are you?'

'I don't *think* so.'

'You don't *think* so?'

'I mean, no. No, we're not.'

'But you said – Oh, forget it. But I would be interested to know how exactly a separated heterosexual man telling his son about a new girlfriend is the equivalent of a guy telling his homophobic dad he's gay. That's problematic on so many levels.'

'I know. It's hard to explain. I'm sorry.'

'I'm sorry too. I'm going now. I need some air.'

'You need some air?'

'I've got to call someone.'

'Who?'

'It's private. Phone me later, if you want.'

'He'll hurt you,' Magali said, when I called to tell her that Robert had said 'I don't *think* so' about going back to his wife. 'You've got to leave him.'

'But I'm in love. I've fallen in love.'

'This is a guy who will hurt you. He doesn't have a clue what he's doing.'

'Nor do I, Mag. I have absolutely no idea.'

I took the Tube south, to walk by the river. I was at Tate Modern when Robert called. He came to meet me and we walked along the South Bank.

I put it to him that his crazy phoning, and his overblown affection right from the start, when he'd plied me with gifts, and said he loved me after only three dates, had been bewildering.

'It was so quick, Robert. You talked about children the first time we slept together. It felt, I don't know, it felt so intense. Here we are, four months on, and you can't even tell your own son about me.'

We stopped and sat on a bench, looking at the Millennium Bridge. I told Robert I'd seen a documentary once, about a man who strung a high wire between the Twin Towers and walked it. The woman he was with at the time was interviewed. They were already lovers when he'd come up with his plan to walk the high wire, and she'd been with him through every stage of its preparation.

As soon as his task was accomplished, he became a world-wide celebrity. In the hours that followed, a woman he'd never met before approached him and told him she wanted him, having seen his stunt. They went to his hotel room and had sex.

In the film, his former lover described how, when they were first together, he had bombarded her with flowers, love letters, small gifts. He had wrapped her into his life, she said, and had expected her to devote herself so completely to him, and to his project, that at no point did he consider that she might have her own destiny to follow. It was, she said, like being harpooned.

'That's how she described it,' I told Robert. 'In this heavy French accent, you know? "*I was com-plet-ly overwhelmed, bowled over, 'arpooned!*" That's what it was like with you, from day one. Being harpooned. If you're still so unsure about us that you can't even tell Philippe I exist, why the thirteen phone calls, just to ask me out for dinner? Why all that crazy stuff at the start? Why did you tell me you loved me, when you'd only just met me?'

'OK,' he said, putting his hands on my shoulders. 'Here's the thing. I had to do those things to know how it would feel. I wasn't sure how I felt about us. How would I, unless I tried it out?' He took his hands away, and he swung one arm on a circuit several times, as though he was about to throw a ball sky-high. 'I needed to get enough velocity to launch us. To put us into orbit, see how we flew up there.'

'So you were faking it?'

'No!'

'What, then?'

'Let's put it another way. In a new relationship, you gotta run it up the flagpole and see if it works.'

'And your feelings? How about trusting your heart?'

'I told you, I don't believe in intuition. I don't want to be guided by my emotions. I've been burned that way before.'

'But you must have a sense of whether you want this thing to carry on.'

'You want a figure? A probability analysis? On a percentage basis, I'd say 70–30.'

'Jesus! No, I don't want a figure. 70–30 what, anyway? Let's stick with the flagpole. If I've understood you correctly, you run it up, this great big flag. You run me up, actually. Let's be honest here. Or the rocket launch. It's *me* you're swinging round and throwing in the air. And I let you do it! I let you throw me as high as you can! And you know what happens when I'm up there? I start to fly. I start to feel things I thought I'd never feel again. I start to come back to life. Then you know what I do? I take the most incredible risk. I climb out of my rocket and I unzip my spacesuit. And you know why? Because I'm falling in love. Because you've made me – I'm – I love you.' Robert stared at me. His eyes were wet. 'Robert, did you even consider the fact that I might fall for what you were telling me?' He was looking at his feet now. 'And what happens then, if you decide it's not the thing for you? What do you do then with your great big flag?'

He put his head in his hands. 'I let it down.'

'And?'

'And I fold it up and put it away.'

'And then?'

'Then I wait. I find another flag, and I try again.'

'That's what you've been doing? Trying me out for size?'

'I don't know.'

'You bastard. You complete and utter bastard.'

'I'm sorry. I really don't know what I've been doing. Not exactly. Will you please let me take you home?'

He bought white roses on the way. We picked up some food, and as soon as we were in, while I put the roses in water, he made dinner.

On my bed, afterwards, we lay looking up at the skylight. I pointed at the white stripes everywhere, and he told me they were called contrails. 'Condensation trails, it's short for. Pilots' footprints. You know, before Galileo set everyone straight, people used to think of air as nothing? As an absence, you know? In actual fact, it weighs a ton.'

Watching the raindrops slide on the glass, I asked him what he wanted from me.

'Everything,' he laughed.

'No, seriously. Why did you start seeing me?'

'We were set up.'

'We were *kind of* set up. But why did you want to keep on seeing me? What was it about me? What made you want to turn it into something? Why have we been doing this?'

'I didn't want to spend Saturday evenings watching *Dexter* on my own.'

'You wanted to watch *Dexter* with me? That's what this is all about? That's what you want from a relationship?'

'I want to be with someone. I want to curl up on the sofa with someone and watch movies. I want to eat breakfast with someone. When I come back from a trip, I want to have someone to talk to about it. After the office, I want to tell someone about my day. About the stuff I see. I see so many things. I have so many things to say. Not important things, you know. Just the little things. Right before I met you, I was beginning to think I might burst with the things I'd seen.'

'Then I came along.'

'Honey, yes you did. And you are so wonderful.'

Later, we did curl up on the sofa and watch a movie. I lay with my eyes closed, thinking about the number of times he'd said the word 'someone', in his speech about what he wanted. For Robert, I realised that evening, it wasn't about me: as long as I was content to inhabit the space he had identified as needing to be filled, I could have been anyone.

After the movie, I was sleepy. Robert was excited by what he called 'our reconciliation', though, and spent an hour drawing up plans for 'our apartment'. I asked him to talk me through it, and he pointed out the long corridor between our rooms.

'I get my own room?'

'Of course.'

'Why? And why so far away?'

'So you can make all the mess you like. I've seen the way you work. This will be a wood finish,' he said, pointing to the kitchen floor. 'And we'll have stone slabs in the main bathroom. A wet room. A huge shower for both of us and a double tub, with wall taps.'

'And carpet, in the bedroom?'

'No way, honey. I'm an American.'

'Well, I'll have it in my room then.'

'Seriously?'

'Seriously. Cream, soft, nubbly carpet.'

'If that's what you want.'

'It's what I want.'

When I knew about my baby coming, I had talked my husband into having a carpet laid in our bedroom. He had resisted the idea, preferring the old, stained floorboards, which we'd uncovered on moving in, and which he liked to walk on, barefoot.

'But look at the nails,' I'd protested.

'There are hardly any. I never feel them.'

'You're not a baby. She'll get splinters, too, when she starts to crawl.'

Pregnant, and dizzy with it, I'd knelt one morning on the new, soft carpet, and pictured her there with me. I lay back and lifted our imaginary girl-child into the air above me, and rolled with her across the room, hearing her laugh. When I did this again, the next morning, I felt her small hands in my hair.

Three months on, when I began to lose her, I stared at the red blood on that cream carpet, and walked away, not wanting to know. As I walked, I left a trail of spots.

'It doesn't matter,' my husband had said that evening when I'd shown him. 'Really, it doesn't matter. We can have it cleaned.'

When I telephoned Susie, she asked how much I was actually losing.

'What?'

'How much blood? A teaspoon? Has there been a teaspoonful yet?'

I looked at the marks on the carpet. 'It's difficult to say.'

'I bled for weeks with Tom. And he was perfectly fine! Not a problem in the slightest. It might be all right, sweetheart. Pop to the doctor and see, but I'm sure it's just a drop. Of course you'll be nervous. Worrying about every little speck of everything that comes out of you. You're going to have a baby. There'll be little spots here and there. It's normal.'

'Half-height or full?' Robert asked. He wanted to know about bookcases, to line that long corridor between our rooms. 'Dark wood or light? Or white plastic! Go super-spacy.'

'How will we do this, though?' I said, my voice barely sounding. 'How will we afford it? Or is it more of your make-believe? Why not settle things with Lena. Why not divorce?'

'OK,' he said. 'I'll have that conversation.'

'You won't.'

'I will. I'll give her a call. I'll say we need to talk.'

'Don't make a promise you can't keep.'

'I promise. Please, though, will you give me some visuals here? Half-height or full, for the corridor bookcases?'

When we were done, he folded away the plans.

'We forgot the trees,' I said.

'Trees?'

'Outside our apartment. All your city plans have trees. I've seen them. Fake trees. Nice green circles. Fake parks. Fake ponds and streets and cars and people. I want us to have some fake trees, with fake birds in.'

'I don't have time to load up the program. You can't do them with pen.'

'I was joking.'

'Oh, OK. It's late, honey. Let's go to bed.'

When the lights were out, I asked him for a story.

'A story about what?' he said, and I curled up against him.

'Anything. Something nice. And set it somewhere I've never been.'

'France?'

'Of course I've been to France.'

'Turkey?'

'No, set it further away. Somewhere a long way away.'

'Japan?'

'Perfect!'

'Ready?'

'Ready.'

He was there for a month, he said, to design an aquarium. It was when he was still young, and he'd rented a small apartment on his own. His neighbour kept birds and sold him one. Robert said he liked its chatter in the mornings, which would otherwise have been lonely. There was a frost, and the bird died. He replaced it straight away, with another from his neighbour, who explained that it was normal, and part of keeping birds, that such things should happen. It was an accident, and he mustn't be deterred. But he might like to keep the window beside the cage closed at night, another time, the neighbour said, if the temperature was set to drop again.

That second bird survived the remainder of Robert's stay, but its chatter was never so friendly, nor its song so sweet. And when Robert opened the door of its cage each morning, ready to refill its feeder and change its little dish of water, and it hopped towards him, he knew it only ever hopped towards him for those things. And when it jumped into his hand and sat there once, quivering, he knew it did so only for warmth, rather than with any real affection.

It took me some time to fall asleep. Thinking of his disappointment that the bird had come to him only for warmth, and food, I remembered again his description of what he wanted from a relationship, when he'd recited his litany of 'someones'. Lying there in bed, listening to his small-cat breathing, it struck me that that was what I'd been to him from the start, when I'd gone to meet him as Susie's stand-in: a someone, filling in for someone else. I wondered then how many relationships were structured in this way, so that people everywhere were doing what Robert had done, and making a life alongside another person without much minding who they were, as long as they filled a gap which would otherwise be empty.

Later that week, Robert met Lena for lunch.

'It was a little hostile,' he said that evening. 'She asked me to state my reasons.'

'Fair enough.'

'Right. She said, "Why should we divorce? We can stay just as we are." So I told her other people are involved now.'

'Oh. And?'

'She cried.'

'Oh.'

'That made me angry.'

'So?'

'So I got angry.'

'Angry how?'

'I said some stuff, you know. Then I didn't like what I was saying so I walked out.'

'*You* didn't like what *you* were saying?'

'Yep.'

'So *you* walked out?

'I'm not proud of it, OK?'

'Did you go back?'

'Nope. I went to the office and called my lawyer.'

The prenup arrived when Robert was at work. I signed for it, then I put it on the breakfast bar and went to the library.

At dinner that evening he offered to read it to me. I said a summary would be fine, and only half listened while he spoke. There were specifics, but I took none of them in. Only one thing stuck in my mind: without recourse to the couple's individual finances, every asset of the marriage would be precisely halved, regardless of which of them had earned it, or purchased it. I zoned out again, as he read a list of what sounded to be exceptions, then I heard his tone change, and realised he had almost finished.

'There's nothing complicated about it. All I want to do now,' he said, folding the paper again, 'is to know that Philippe is happy, and to buy a place in London. Settle down, finally.'

At his apartment near Angel, there were several paintings of clapboard houses in Maine. A model house, cast in clay, stood on a bookcase. Individual wooden letters – H, O, M, E – stood side by side in the entrance hall.

Before their marriage, when Lena's mother had insisted on the prenup and had had it drawn up, Robert had barely paid attention.

'Everyone was doing it then,' he said. 'Everyone in New York, I mean. All of Lena's friends, that's what she said. Her mother is a wealthy Swedish feminist. She wanted to look after her daughter. It was no big deal.'

When he saw his own lawyer, though, he was told to think carefully before entering into the agreement.

'Why?' he'd replied, without having read it. 'We're going into this forever. Give me your pen. Where do I sign?'

Talking to me, he remembered how, on the morning of the wedding, he'd captained the *Osedda* and sailed his mother and his sister to Lena's family's property at Maine. His mother, standing with him at the helm, had said, 'Be careful not to rely on all this. None of it belongs to you.'

'But it's mine, Mom. Don't you understand? I'll never have to worry about money again.'

Robert sat with me in the apartment on the day the prenup had arrived, holding it. Made up of just a few manila pages, it was hole-punched and bound together with lawyers' pink ribbon.

'When I read this this evening, that's what I thought of. I thought of what my mom said, and the look on her face when she said it. I'm gonna call my sister. She'll know what to do.'

While I washed up from dinner, Robert Skyped Charlotte. The conversation came down from the mezzanine, so I heard her advise Robert to do as Lena had suggested, and stay as he was.

'Why divorce?' Charlotte asked. 'It's expensive, cutting everything in two. Come to an arrangement about property, and live like a free man.' She and her movie-producer husband could invite him to parties, where they would introduce him to people. 'No cameras!' she laughed. 'So no one needs to know what you do, or with who!'

'How was it?' I said later, in bed.

'Oh, inconsequential.'

'I could hear. I was right downstairs from you! You were both shouting!'

'She told me to have some fun,' he said, laughing. 'Play the field. Throw away constraint. She said, why divorce, if it's going to be a fuss?'

Before we went to sleep, he held me, and talked some more about his lunch with Lena.

'Perhaps we should've arranged a third party to be there with us.'

'Like who?'

'A mediator. I could've booked our counsellor, the marriage guidance woman we were seeing. That's what Lena did. That's how she got it together to tell me she wanted a separation.'

'She told you in a session?'

'Halfway through. Came out of nowhere. I literally couldn't believe it. I literally couldn't take it in.'

'Really?

'Really.'

'But you knew she wasn't happy with the way things were between you?'

'Things were OK!'

'You hadn't had sex for years. You told me!'

'I figure she'd have said if she wanted any.'

'You don't think she was getting it somewhere else?'

'She wouldn't have done something like that. She just wouldn't.'

'So she was perfectly happy to go without. She's an attractive, healthy, middle-aged woman, and she has no interest whatsoever in sex. Run that by me again, would you?'

'Hmmm. You don't know her.' He picked up *Train Dreams*, and we didn't talk about it any more.

Eventually, after we'd fucked, harder and for longer than we had done for a while, I switched out the lights, and asked if there was anything he wanted to say.

'Well,' he began. 'You know what you said about me knowing she wasn't happy with the way things were between us?'

'Hm-mmm.'

'There was this one time, she cried, for absolutely no reason, like some terrible thing had happened.'

'When?'

'Two, three years ago maybe. It was a Saturday night. I was getting my bike ready for the morning. I didn't think of it at the time, but now ...'

'Now what?'

Saturday nights, he said, he would stand his racer against the wall in the corridor outside their bedroom. Fixing his pump to one tyre, then the other, he'd inflate them for his long Sunday-morning ride. Because he wanted to avoid stopping on the way and holding up the other guys, he would make them as hard as was safe. Once when he was doing this, pumping so fast he was sweating, he heard what sounded like a yell from the bedroom, and went in.

'She was lying on the bedcover, totally undressed. Her face was soaked. Buckets of tears. I asked her what the matter was, and she just stared at me and said, "Don't you know? Don't you know anything?"'

'Oh, Robert,' I said.

'What?'

'You are so idiotic.'

Early one Sunday morning, he'd left me sleeping and gone to get ready for his ride. Woken by a noise from the corridor, I wrapped the sheet around me and went to see.

He was naked, and his breathing was quick. I watched his arse and his thrusting arm and I listened to him panting. I put a hand on his back. With two fingers, I took some of the juice which had run onto my inner thigh and reached round to put it in his mouth.

'You can swim in me. I'm so wet you can swim in me.'

He turned, and lifted me onto him. I wrapped my legs round his back and he carried me to the kitchen. I whispered, 'We can make a child, now. This morning. I'm ovulating. I can feel it.'

He kissed my hand, and bit it lightly. 'I don't know.'

'But you might.'

'I might.' He raised me onto the breakfast bar, and laid me back, flat. He pulled up my knees, then my legs, into the air. 'What day are you on?'

'What do you mean?'

'On your cycle?'

'Twelve, maybe eleven.'

'Let's try it without.'

'You told me you'd say, if you knew you didn't want kids. So does this mean you do?'

He moved in, and placed my calves and feet behind his neck. I could feel his hands underneath, lifting me. Then he was holding himself, rubbing himself, using himself to stroke me, beginning to slip himself inside me.

'Let's do it, honey. I know you want it without. I can feel it.'

'And if I conceive, and you decide you don't want a child?'

'There are things you can do.'

'What things?'

'You know what I mean.'

I sat up and pushed him away. Getting down from the surface, I pulled the sheet around myself. 'Go and have a shower.'

'Jesus, honey – look at me!' He was half shouting, and holding himself.

In the operating theatre, before I went under, the anaesthetist was late. When she came, she was out of breath. She held her clipboard up and said, after the name checks and date of birth checks and blood pressure checks were done, 'Termination?'

'I'm sorry?'

She pulled down her glasses and looked at me.

'I have to check. Formalities.'

'Yes, but what did you say?'

'Termination.' She looked back at her clipboard. 'You're here for an abortion? You don't want this child.'

When I cried out and stood up, a nurse came in and held me. It was a mistake, she explained. 'We know you're not here for an abortion. We know, sweetheart. It's OK.'

I asked to see the form, the second time, when they'd calmed me. 'It's important,' I said. 'It's important you don't put "termination".'

'We haven't. Look, here's what it says now.'

Underneath the acronym, the words were spelled out: 'Evacuation of retained products of conception.'

'It makes a difference, do you see?' I said to the anaesthetist. 'I'm not choosing this. I wanted my child. I wanted my baby. Do you understand?'

'Yes. I do.'

I didn't want to look at her, and kept my eyes shut while she started.

I think of Robert less often now. When I do, he comes to mind as a guy I slept with for a time, and had thought I'd maybe stay with for longer. Thinking back, I wonder why it had been so easy for me to become his 'someone'. What it was about me that made me so capable of climbing into the space he had prescribed. And why, when it came to the end, I found it so hard to step out of it.

My father was a banker.

When women began showing up in his office as colleagues, rather than secretaries, he pronounced the situation absurd. The first time a female director attended a meeting of the bank's board, he left work early.

At the family supper table that evening, he described the scene for us as a comedy. My mother, whom he preferred not to take paid employment, lest it reflect poorly on his ability to support his wife and family, broke for just one second from her task of serving our casserole, but said nothing at all.

My brother, Will, who is a year and a half younger than me, had a set of keys cut for the front and back doors of our family house on his fourteenth birthday. I was at university by the time I had a set of keys of my own, and even then, they were for my college rooms, rather than for our family home.

On Will's seventeenth birthday, when one of his presents from my parents was a series of driving lessons, I asked my mother and father for lessons of my own. Their response was to leave a brochure for classes at Leiths School on my dressing table, with the pages turned over to mark the ones she and my father were prepared to give me for my nineteenth birthday. It would be fun, she said, to learn how to cook properly, and they'd sounded ever so nice when she'd phoned. When I settled down with someone, and was building a home, I would need to know how to do dinner parties, not just the everyday.

I asked my father for a second opinion. He told me that they had already discussed the question of a Leiths course, which they had both agreed was a perfectly adequate present. On this, he said, as was the case with every aspect of my upbringing, they were as one. When I asked him one last time about driving lessons, his surprise seemed entirely genuine.

'But why would *you* need to drive, Lizzie-bee? You can walk to lectures at college, or cycle. When you're at home with us, you never go anywhere apart from orchestra rehearsals, and piano lessons. Returning your books to the library, that sort of thing. We're always happy to take you. You know we are. All you have to do is ask, darling.'

When Robert came back from his cycle ride that Sunday afternoon, he held me until I asked to be let go. He said he was sorry for having pushed me on birth control. He knew we had a deal, and he knew he'd crossed the line. It wouldn't happen again, unless he made up his mind. Then he held me some more, harder and for longer, until I said, 'Robert, I need to pee. Stop it. You're squeezing me.'

All afternoon, he worked on his laptop, up on the mezzanine. I lay on the daybed beside him, and read.

He finished his work, then pulled me up from the daybed. Slowly, he undressed me and laid me out on the floor. He was fully clothed and he knelt over me, inspecting my body.

'Robert,' I said, pulling at his shirt, 'this is weird.'

'I want to see you properly.' He tucked his shirt back in. 'I want to see all of you. I want to know you.'

He inspected my nipples then he traced their shape with his fingers. He moved my legs apart and knelt slightly in front of me. He brought his face into me. Touching me with his tongue, lightly, he drew back and looked again, like an artist or a student of anatomy.

I sighed, half in complaint, half in pleasure. He brought his face closer and started licking me, then he took my hand and made me touch myself while he licked me, or licked my hand.

When I sighed again he sat back up. He looked at all the parts of my body. Laying his palm flat where mine had been, he rubbed me.

'Submit,' he said, rubbing and looking. 'Submit.'

I started to cry, then I came.

April

<u>How to tell how much daylight remains</u>

If you are out on a boat, and you need to know how much daylight remains: 1. Fully extend your arm in front of you, with your hand rotated thumb-side up. 2. Bend your hand at the wrist so that your hand is now at right-angle to your extended arm, with the palm now facing you. 3. Tuck your thumb down. 4. With one eye closed, align the bottom of your hand with the horizon line. If the horizon line is obscured, use your judgement and put the bottom of your hand where the horizon should be. 5. Keeping one eye closed, estimate how many hand breadths there are between the horizon line and the bottom of the sun's arc. 6. Each hand breadth equals one hour left of daylight.

Frank Johnson, *Sailing by Hand, A Beginner's Manual*

I was invited to spend Easter with my brother and his family in Norfolk.

'They said I can bring you,' I told Robert. 'If we want.'

'Could we stay in town?'

'What, ask them to come here?'

'No, honey. Just us, please? Just you and me.'

'It's a time for being with people. It's a holiday. A time for feasting.'

'We are people.'

'Can you commit, though?'

'Give me the dates and I'll commit. What kind of feasting?'

He'd stuck to the deal we had made at the beginning, over our tea at Tate Modern: to cook at home as often as we ate out. Initially, he met his obligation by decanting high-end ready meals into pans, and half passing them off as his own.

Once, I came in from the library and heard him in the kitchen. It was dark outside, and he was reflected in the long tall windows at the other end of the open-plan, which meant I could see him clearly, though he couldn't see me. He was poised in front of the work surface, one arm raised as though to take an ingredient from the shelf. He stayed quite still, and shook his head in irritation. When I called out, 'Hi, honey, I'm home,' and stepped into the room, it was as though I had snapped a clapperboard shut and said, 'Kitchen, Scene 1, Take 3.'

Reaching his arm higher, he took a packet of rice from the cupboard, saying casually, over his shoulder, 'Hey there. I'm just cooking.'

After a few weeks, I asked if he'd like to try cooking from scratch, with raw ingredients.

'It's easier like this, don't you think?' Then he demonstrated, sliding chicken cubes in pepper sauce from a plastic sleeve, which he threw in the bin. 'No chopping. No mess. No equipment!'

When he put in his request for Easter in London, I told him I would cook an Easter lunch. For that, I said, we would have to address the equipment issue: it was time to go shopping.

'For what?'

'Kitchen things. Don't panic. You don't have to come. I'll get them.'

'No way,' he said. 'My kitchen, my things.'

In a kitchenware department on Oxford Street, he said that whatever came into his apartment had to be black, or navy blue or white. Beyond that, the choices were all mine. He was happy to simply pay, and to carry the tea towels, Sabatier knife set, apron, chopping boards, steamer, oven gloves and, at the last, a roasting tray.

Persuading him to replace the bedspread was more difficult.

'It's stained, Robert. Big stains, of indeterminate origin.'

'Those are Bella-stains.'

'Your dog slept on this?'

'She slept with us, usually. Or on us.'

'Us?'

'Lena and me.'

We tried out several, but in the end chose none of them. There were playful photographs: him hiding under a coverlet, one red-socked foot poking out and resting on the floor. The two of us shot from above, side by side on the mocked-up bed, our faces on the pillows. When I pulled off my T-shirt and his, and took another shot with our bare shoulders showing, as if, under the blanket, we were naked, he called time on the game.

For the duvet, he insisted on goose down, even when I pointed out the price. 'It's an investment,' he said. 'We're home-building.'

A week on, I checked in with him again. 'I'm happy to stay here with you for Easter, but not if you're going to bail on me.'

'Why would I? You gave me the dates. We scheduled it.'

'Won't you need to be "available" in case Philippe –? What's he doing for Easter?'

'Staying in the US. Lena's going over. Honey, quit worrying. We'll do something fun, the two of us.'

'We'll do Easter.'

'What, you're a Christian all of a sudden?'

'No.'

'So why do we have to "do" Easter? Let's just have a nice weekend.'

'It matters to me. It's a ritual. I like Easter. I like Christmas. I like Halloween and Bonfire Night. I like Advent. I like Christmas carols and Christmas trees and wrapping up presents and making mince pies. I like hiding chocolate eggs. I like roasting a chicken and baking a cake and toasting hot cross buns. It's something to celebrate.'

'What are you celebrating if you're not a Christian?'

'It's just a thing. You get to the end of Lent and you eat eggs and chicken and chocolate. I can't believe I have to explain. You're an educated guy. You've been living here eight years. Anyway, I'm your girlfriend. Why question me?'

He was laughing. 'What did you give up for Lent?' He put out his hand but I didn't take it.

'Nothing.'

He pulled me in and pressed his face to the top of my head and breathed into my hair, 'I love it when you're mad at me.' He kissed my neck and put a tongue to my ear and licked it, sliding one hand up and under my top and undoing my bra, and the other into my knickers. I was wet straight away. He put a finger inside me and slowly took it out. 'I won't bail on you. You can tell your brother you're not coming.'

I stood on my tiptoes to kiss him. 'I have already.'

I found out there would be an Easter market at Columbia Road. It would be the flower market, the same as every week, people struggling with bundles of lilies, and plants almost too tall to be carried. But there would be extras: Easter food stalls, a magician and a jazz band.

'Have you been there before?' I asked him.

'I have not.'

'Then you should. People come from all over town. We should. But there's no point going after half eight, really.'

'Why?'

'Too crowded. Can't see anything, can't move.'

'OK. It's a plan.'

Nearer the time, I suggested we stay at our own places the night before, and I'd meet him at the Tube around 7 a.m. 'We can walk there together. It'll be like one of our dates, in the early days.'

'Honey! You have to stay at mine.'

'I'll be tired. I'm working really hard this week. I'll just want to sleep on my own.'

I let him talk me into staying at his, but when it came to it, I took my things up to the mezzanine and made a space on the daybed. He said he was OK with it, but after an hour he woke me up.

'I just don't get it. I'm sorry, I can't do this. We should sleep in the same bed. We're a couple.'

'You just woke me up!'

'I know.'

Back in his bed, I tried to explain. I said that for centuries, couples slept in separate beds unless they had to share, for reasons of space. 'Montaigne writes about it,' I said, explaining that the writer and his wife had their own beds at quite opposite ends of the same house, and came together in one of them only for lovemaking. 'Sleep is such a private thing, Robert.'

'I'm not Montaigne. Nor are you, kiddo. I wanna sleep next to you.'

So I told him then, what I'd been trying to keep back, that the fact I shared his bed as often as I did was surprising to me. That he was the first man I'd been able to sleep a whole night through with since the end of my marriage. But that, sometimes, the idea of it was too much, and too strange, and that this was one of those nights. That I didn't know why, but I thought it might have something to do with having, for so many years, known only the shape of one man's back against my stomach. Only having opened my eyes in the morning to the smell of one man's skin. Only having been asked by one man, each night before falling asleep, which way I wanted to be held. Only having been brought from a bad dream by one person, who, later, by agreeing to be left when I said I had to leave him, had set me adrift on a wide ocean. And that, given the choice, I would prefer not to share my bed with anyone new, though I wanted more than anything to be held at night, and not to wake alone.

'But I need you, Elizabeth. You have to let me need you.'

'For everything? Can't you sleep this one night without me?'

'You've just told me a story. Let me tell you one in return.'

Soon after his split from Lena he'd gone to Frankfurt for a conference. He was using the hotel gym on the third day when he found himself unable to move.

'I had no idea where I was, or even what I was. I couldn't move my arms, my legs. I was standing on a running machine and I didn't know how to get off it. I knew I was in a foreign country, but at that moment, I could've been in a hotel gym anywhere, and I could have been anyone. All I knew was that I was completely, totally alone.' He rubbed his eyes, and I saw that he was crying. 'You've changed that. I need you, do you see? I need you, so that I know where I am, and so that I know I'm really here.'

At Columbia Road in the morning, he found a small gift shop. He chose a silver ring and wanted to buy it for me.

'I always lose jewellery. Always. I'd feel terrible if you gave me this and I lost it.'

'So let me buy it, then if you lose it you can pay me. How about that?'

'That's just weird. Then I'd be paying you as a punishment. You are so weird, you know that? It's a nice ring. I like it. If you hadn't shown me it, I'd have chosen it anyway. I'll get it. If you want to buy a present, buy something for yourself.'

We separated for a while, so he could choose his present. Wandering the flower stalls, I bought bundles of daffodils and narcissi for his apartment. From one of the Easter stands, I bought a bag of chocolate eggs, cast in pastel-coloured sugar shells the size of duck eggs. When he found me, later, I was listening to the jazz band. I didn't hear him at first, or at least, I could hear what sounded like his voice but didn't make the connection. When he said 'Lena' a second time, I looked again and saw it was him, coming towards me. I wasn't sure which of us was more embarrassed by his slip. Taking my arm, he looked not at me but away, and I realised he'd decided to pretend it hadn't happened.

He wouldn't say what he'd chosen. At the apartment again, he unwrapped three small model houses, made from sheets of reddened tin, and placed them on his desk on the mezzanine.

He took his time doing it. In the kitchen, I began to slice an onion but he heard me and ran down. He wanted to cook, he said. It was the christening of his new equipment, and it would be a pleasure for him. He asked me to talk him through the recipes, then he tied his new apron on, and I left him.

While he worked, I went around the apartment hiding the chocolate eggs I'd bought. In three of the places I chose, I found eggs he'd already hidden, and realised why he'd been so long with the model houses.

He was still chopping, so I stayed on the mezzanine to Skype my brother and his family. In Norfolk, the sun was shining. Will carried his iPad into the garden, where the children were hunting eggs, the two of them chasing and screaming and jumping into flower beds, so that Will's wife ran from the house, laughing, and told them not to step on her azaleas.

'Where are you?' Will called out. 'Are you with your deal-maker? Freeze any eggs yet? Can we meet him?'

'Don't call him that,' I whispered, frowning.

I took my laptop to the kitchen, and Robert had his first conversation with my family: aproned, red in the face, and chewing on a carrot, he stared at my brother. 'Who he?' he said.

'Oh! I'm sorry. Will, this is Robert. Robert, Will.'

My brother grinned, then just as Robert began to say 'Hello', he disappeared from the screen, tackled to the ground by his younger son, Albert, who jumped back up and asked me if I'd found all my eggs yet.

'Not quite. Let's go see if we can find the last one, hey?' I left Robert in the kitchen, and carried the laptop back upstairs. I showed Albert one of the eggs I'd hidden for Robert, and put my fingers to my lips. 'Don't tell.'

'Who's that?'

'Who?'

'In the photo, Auntie Lizzie. On the bookshelf.'

I'd forgotten about Lena. I reached behind me and put the photo of her and Philippe face down. 'Oh, just a friend of Robert's,' I said, swinging the laptop away. 'No one important.'

Later, after we'd found our chocolate eggs, and eaten our feast, Robert said he wanted to FaceTime Philippe, and asked, would I mind taking a short walk?

'Now?'

'Yep.'

'On my own?'

'It's just less complicated that way, you know.'

'What way?'

'If you're somewhere else. I usually show him the apartment when we FaceTime, if he asks.'

As I let myself out, I heard the call begin.

'Oh, hey, nothing much,' Robert said. 'It's just a lazy Sunday. I took a look at a market this morning. It was fun. Bought myself a present. Then I came back and hung out, made myself some lunch. What about you, dude? Are you with your mom?'

The week after Easter, I had a small operation. A tiny internal tear had opened up in my stomach wall, roughly at my midriff. Some days, it hurt a little, and from time to time, there was a sort of 'pop', and a piece of muscle emerged which shouldn't have done. By pressing it lightly, I could push it back in. On seeing a surgeon, I'd been told that either I could live with the sensation and forget about it, or, and this was his advised course of action, I could have a small piece of mesh inserted, and held in place with permanent stitches. As long as I was aware of the risk of leaving it, which was that, one day, the opening might increase enough for part of my intestine to become strangulated, and cause my death, the choice was mine.

My operation was booked for the middle of the month.

'It's minor,' I told Robert on the phone in Canada.

'But what's it called?' he shouted. He was at the side of the road, somewhere north of Alberta. 'It must have a name. Why didn't you tell me about it before? This is kind of short notice!'

'Oh. It's an umbilical hernia. It happened when I was born, apparently, and it's opened up again. They don't know why. It was arranged forever ago. Yes, it's open surgery, and yes, it's a general. But it's no big deal, really.'

He said I should find out everything I could, nonetheless, and make an informed decision about whether to go through with it.

'Of course I'm going through with it! Are you crazy?'

In the days leading up to the surgery, Robert sent me YouTube footage of the procedure. I watched two minutes of the first clip, and asked him not to send me any more.

'I'm just trying to help, honey. You should be as clued up as possible about what they're going to do to you in there!'

'Yeah, but I don't need to actually see it. It's like a horror movie, that thing you sent. How could you?'

'I was trying to help. I feel bad. I'm so far away.'

'Well, don't feel bad! Or come back and help, if you do!'

He took me at my word, and flew in the day before.

Assuming I would want him to escort me to the hospital and collect me, he went ahead and booked a cab. When I told him I'd prefer to take Magali up on her offer of coming with me, and taking me back to stay at hers for the night, he insisted.

'How's she going to do that? What about Olivier? What about the club?'

'Olivier's a grown-up. He's cool with it. And the club has staff, you know!'

We argued a little, and he insisted.

When I came round from the anaesthetic I was taken to a side room, where I fell asleep again. Later, I opened my eyes to find Robert's phone in front of my face.

'Smile.' There was a click, and I blacked out again.

Waking a second time, I was too spacy to say anything to him about the camera. He looked crestfallen, and told me the nurse had asked him not to take photographs.

'I'm not surprised,' I said quietly. 'Are you?'

When he emailed the image to me, a few days later, I looked like all of my friends had, in their new-baby photos from the delivery room: the hospital gown sat lightly on me, and I was bleary-eyed and pale. The only difference was the absence of a child, and the fact I looked frightened, rather than happy.

I didn't acknowledge his email, and he never asked about it. That day, as soon as I'd peed, we were allowed to leave the hospital. At the apartment, he paid the cab driver, and helped me in. When I was settled on the sofa, wrapped in Lena's fur throw, he said he was going out and would be back in half an hour. 'Definitely no more than one hour, max, or two. You just call me, honey, if there's anything you need!'

'You can't leave!'

'We need food.'

'No, I mean you *actually* can't leave. That's the whole point. That's the deal. I came round from a general exactly three hours ago. You signed a form to say you'd stay with me for twenty-four hours. That's the only reason they let me –'

'We just need a few things, for dinner. For breakfast! We need milk, and I should get some soup for you. Something light, for when you're ready to eat.'

'You didn't think of going before?'

'Before what?'

'Before you came to get me from the hospital.'

'I was at the office. Actually, I need to stop in there now, if that's OK. There's a conference call I should be on. It'll be quick, I promise. Then I'll go to the store and come back. Please don't be dramatic about it. There really is no other way.'

When he'd gone, I called Magali.

'Why didn't you stay with me, honey?' she said. 'Shall I come over right now? I can come over. You need to think about this guy, seriously. Is he the guy you want to be with? Is he the guy you want to have a kid with?'

'Hey. Easy.'

'I'm sorry. I don't want to break your balls, sweetie, but if Olivier ever did something like that to me. Oh boy. You want me to come over right now?'

'No.' By now I was crying. 'I'm OK, I guess. Maybe tomorrow, if Olivier's around to cover.'

'Sure thing. No question. Tomorrow, noon. I'll pick you up and bring you here. We'll get you right, and get you home, then, babe, you know what?'

'You're going to quote a musical at me, aren't you?'

'I haven't quite said this before, girl. I've bided my time, seeing you try so hard to make this work. But here goes.' She was singing then, and I laughed a little. 'You've got to wash this man right out of your hair.' She sang the rest, then she said, 'He doesn't make you smile, you know? He doesn't make you laugh.'

I went to Magali's the next day. Robert was due to fly to Alberta again, in any case. As I was packing my bag, he said he'd be back the following weekend, and would book us a table for lunch.

'I'll take you somewhere special, honey. A recuperation date.'

When Magali arrived, he smiled, and seemed not to notice that she'd kept her sunglasses on and wasn't smiling back.

In the mornings, Magali was in her office on the top floor, working through menus and accounts, putting in food orders for the club. Olivier cooked lunch for the three of us, then in the afternoons, I slept. While one of them was at the club, I watched movies with the other, and went to bed early.

One evening, I helped Olivier to wash up.

'You stayed with this man for a child, right?'

'Is that what Magali told you?'

'We don't see why else. He talks about his wife as though he's still with her. He doesn't make you laugh. And he tells you what to do the whole time.'

'I've been lonely, these years.'

'Magali said you sounded lonely, when you called her to come and get you.'

'I was. He had to work. It was a misunderstanding.'

'It would be hard, I think, to have a child with someone who doesn't know how to care for anyone.'

'He has been loving. I mean, he's in love with me. It's been nice.'

'And he wants to control you, I think. Magali tells me that. I can see it for myself, but she tells me. Is it time to stop with this man, do you think? Why would you want to be with someone like that?'

I could think of nothing to say, and didn't answer. He apologised, and said perhaps he'd gone too far. He held me, and I told him not to be sorry.

'Now what?' I said.

'A movie? Some tea? What would you like to watch?'

'I think I'll just fall asleep. But yes, let's. You choose, I'll watch with my eyes closed.'

After five days, I asked Olivier to take me home.

I still wasn't comfortable walking, so I took a cab to the small Italian restaurant Robert had booked for us in Marylebone. As I pulled up outside, and saw him standing on the pavement, I decided to break things off.

At first, we were strangers.

'It's my stitches,' I said, shying away from his embrace.

By the second course, though, he had made me laugh, and soon I was asking him to stop.

'They'll come undone. Please, stop.'

Soon, I had forgotten everything, and was enjoying the new distance. Maybe, I thought, this was all that had been needed. A standing away, and a recalibration.

Afterwards, we waited for the bill, and he handed me a small object.

'I wanted to keep it back, you know.'

'What is it?'

'It's a gift. Open it.'

'Here?'

'Right here.'

It was a bottle of expensive scent, the kind advertised by movie stars, in heavy-paged haute couture magazines. It was a scent I'd never owned, and it was the first time a man had given me anything like it.

'Thank you. I mean, it's gorgeous. What do you mean, keep it back?'

'I wanted to see how things went today. You seemed kind of mad at me last week, after your op. I didn't know if it was the drugs you were on, or what. Do you know, I was even kind of worried you were going to tell me you didn't want to see me again!'

'We do need to talk, Robert.'

'Now?'

'No. I've booked a cab. It'll be here any minute. I can see you tomorrow, if you want. There are some things I need to say to you. I don't think I can do this any more.'

'This?'

'Us.'

'What do you mean, us?'

'I'm so sorry,' then the waiter was telling me my cab was outside, and Robert was standing to help me. 'You know it won't work, Robert. We both know it.'

He held the restaurant door, and shook his head. 'Don't do this, Elizabeth. Not now. Not like this.'

'Goodbye, Robert.'

'You said you'd see me tomorrow. Will you come over?'

'Let's meet in town.' I was in the cab now, drawing my feet up, holding his gift against my stitches. 'Somerset House. There's a coffee shop, just where you come in. The top corner of the courtyard. I'll be there at eleven,' then we were pulling away, and he was waving.

I slept badly. My stitches hurt, and when I looked, the bruising had spread, and was yellowing. I sat at the dining table and looked out. There was a couple by the launderette, kissing, for what seemed like forever. The woman pulled away, then the man pulled her in again and she laughed, and they began again. When the street was empty, at 2 a.m., or 3, I went up and tried once more to sleep. I was wide awake, though, bothered by the memory of my conversation with Olivier, when I'd helped him with the washing-up and he had asked me why I wanted to be with someone who controlled me.

That evening, I had been unable to find an answer to his question.

Now, though, thinking about the couple outside the launderette, kissing, and imagining myself being alone again, without Robert, I found my answer, with a horrible, startling clarity. I wanted to be with Robert, not only despite his need to control me, but also because of it. It made it easier, being controlled. It made it easier to be sure I was loved. If someone was always there, wanting me there, wanting me to be a certain way, and wanting me to be with them wherever they went, there was no doubt about their feelings for me.

At 5 a.m. I woke from a dream about Robert, and was scared, suddenly, that if I told him I'd changed my mind, and asked him to have me back, he might refuse.

At 6 a.m. I texted, knowing his phone would be off and he'd read it when he got up.

Had an idea. I'll swing by yours and pick you up. You're on the way, anyway. So don't go. Don't go until I get there.

I stopped at the flower stall opposite my apartment.

'Is it for a special occasion?' the boy said.

'Yes.'

'Who for?'

'It's complicated.'

'Try me. It's my job. It's for a guy, right?'

I blushed, thinking of Magali and Olivier. 'Yesterday he was my boyfriend.'

'Aha.'

'I told him I didn't want to see him any more.'

'I'll see what I can do. These, I think, miss. These are a good place to start.'

An hour later, instead of using my keys, I rang Robert's bell. He buzzed me up but when I reached his apartment and knocked, he didn't come. I waited, then I knocked again and saw the door was ajar.

There was music from the bedroom. I stood in the doorway and watched.

He was on the bed, sewing on a button. His foot was tapping, and he sang along, quietly.

I phoned Magali in the afternoon. I said it had nearly killed me, finding him like that.

'He was like a boy,' I said. Taken unawares, I explained, he'd seemed so gentle, and so content. 'That was when I knew.'

'Knew what?'

'I just knew. I didn't want to hurt him. I didn't want to lose him.'

'It was deliberate,' she said. 'He set it up!'

'How? He didn't even know I was there.'

'He buzzed you in. He left the door unlocked. He chose the music. Sewing? Since when have you ever seen Robert sew on a button? You are so completely gullible, Elizabeth. This guy is playing you like a guitar. That's all he's ever done. Think about it!'

'I guess,' I said. 'So –'

'So?'

'It still nearly killed me.'

'Elizabeth. Please.'

'What?'

'Please don't tell me you screwed him.'

I put my hand over the phone.

'Elizabeth? Say something!'

Watching him sew his button, I had made a noise. He'd turned, and smiled. Standing up, he took the white roses.

'Come,' I said, and he followed.

On the mezzanine, he undid my dress.

'You're wearing the perfume.'

'I'm wearing the perfume.'

He sat up on the daybed and lifted me onto his lap, barely touching me.

'It's fine,' I said. 'I'm not made of glass.'

'I'm being careful. I'm trying to be careful.'

He undid my bra, and cupped my breasts. He was inside me then, and his face was at my neck. Barely moving, I came. He held me, and stayed quite still.

'Honey?' I whispered. 'Did you −?'

'It's OK. I don't want to hurt you.' He placed a hand on my belly, just above my stitches, then he laid his head on my shoulder. 'Thank you.'

'For what?'

'Thank you for coming back to me.'

I stayed with him that night. On the sofa, before we went to bed, he told me that when he'd learned to pilot a plane, he was told that the most important rule, the one that would save his life, was this.

Your instruments are your window on reality.

In order to survive, you need to understand the data they provide, and ignore any sensory message which suggests otherwise.

'That's what I learned. Following my heart would literally kill me. This is a terrifying situation to be in. I'm going against everything I've learned.'

Later, we slept together in his bed. I was most comfortable curled up on my side, my hands on his back, him facing away from me.

'You are my lighter,' he whispered.

'Your what?'

'I am a yacht at harbour. You are a small boat attached to me by a little length of rope. You're how my captain goes to and fro, if he wants to walk on land.'

As my breathing slowed, he told me we had just returned from a long sea journey. We had made land, and night had fallen.

'You're not a yacht,' I breathed. 'And I'm not your lighter. I'm a person, not a boat. You can be the captain. I'm your deckhand.'

'OK,' he said. 'Cute deckhand. Wanna share my cabin?'

'Sure. What happens next?'

We had cleaned our boat, he said, and re-provisioned her. The sail was furled and the deck swept. There were only the sound of a rope straining, or of other boats, rocking. We were sharing a tiny cabin, just the two of us, and in the morning, if we wanted, we would be gone early, before anyone else was even awake, so that it would be as though we'd never been there. Within a half-hour, he said, we could be on the high seas, but for now, we were sleeping, and dreaming of what we had seen on our voyage, out in the big blue nowhere.

May

How to make an SOS call from a plane

The question from air traffic is not 'How many people are on board?' but, rather, 'How many souls?' In answer to the former iteration, there would always be an ambiguity; should it be 'Eight' or 'Me plus seven'? But to the question 'How many souls?' there is no doubt: the answer should be 'Eight'.

Martha Parker, *The Language of Flight*

As a student Robert drew angels, which he fashioned into models with stiff card. He graduated to ply-board frames, and clad them with thin sheets of aluminium. Once, he constructed an angel from strips of wire, clad with nothing at all. Forming the fancy that it might take flight, he remade the hollow prototype several times and consulted aviation manuals. His last attempt was the biggest: at twenty foot tall it stood lightly, but he went no further with the idea.

When he completed the foundation course, his grand-mother booked him a series of lessons at an airfield in New Jersey. He learned to fly, and the angels stopped. Finding himself unable to let go of that last vast figure, he stored it in a friend's studio.

'You're like one of my angels,' he said to me one Saturday in May. Smiling, he held the fabric of my top between his fingers. 'I'm sorry, have you been here long? Were you bored out of your mind?'

'No,' I said. 'It's been fine. I watched the water. I watched people.'

'I've never seen this before,' he said, holding the fabric again. 'Is it new?'

We were at Victoria Park for a picnic. The polka-dot top he'd admired was made to a simple design: two large T-shaped cotton panels stitched together, with ribbons attached on either side at waist height. If the ribbons were left untied, the top hung slack. This morning I'd tied them, so the fabric was cinched at my waist and fell in folds.

Waiting for him to arrive, I'd taken off my backpack and stood facing the lake. The breeze was from both sides. Beneath the ribbon ties, the fabric of my top was lifted up and out. The sleeves had billowed like wings, and I could feel the air on my tummy.

'You really like it?' I said. 'I was going to send it to the charity shop.' I untied the ribbons and held the fabric out in front. 'Then I thought it might come in handy.' Puffing my cheeks, I thrust my belly forward until Robert laughed.

'I'm not joking!' I said, laughing as well. 'I mean it. It's basically a maternity top.' I held the fabric out again. 'Look!'

He picked up my backpack and moved off. 'Come on, honey. I'm hungry. Let's eat.'

Laying out the lunch, he said it was his first ever picnic.

'It can't be.' I unpacked cutlery and plates, and small glass tumblers for the wine.

'In London.'

'In eight years?'

'That's right.'

'You guys never –?'

'Nope.'

'But why?'

'It's not something we would have done.' He took a baguette from his bag. 'Lena would never have – I guess Philippe might've liked it.'

'Of course he would! Look!' There were families all around us. Holding up blankets and letting them settle, they opened bags of food. One or two groups had lit tiny barbecue trays and were sticking sausages onto skewers.

'Well,' he said, pulling out a half-bottle of red wine, 'I have some catching up to do.'

He asked a passer-by to take our photograph. Kneeling up behind me, he clasped me in his arms and posed for the shot with his chin on the top of my head. Later, he went to the drinks kiosk. I'd brought the weekend papers, and when he reappeared with little cardboard cups of coffee, I was buried in an article.

'You don't want to talk?' he frowned.

'We talked a lot over lunch,' I said. 'Let's read.'

'Seriously?'

'Seriously.'

He knelt down, then he pointed at a couple to our left. They held novels, and sat back-to-back, with their torsos resting against each other. 'They've obviously been together forever,' he said.

'Hmm?'

'They must've been. It takes years for couples to be able to read together.'

'Honey, come on.' I passed him the news section. 'It's the weekend. It's a nice thing to do.'

He objected a little more then he was quiet. Every now and again he told me about an article. I read out extracts of a profile of a writer I knew, or a review of a play I wanted us to see. Then he said, 'I still can't believe it just disappeared. It's impossible.'

'Hmmm?'

'A whole goddam jet. Two hundred and thirty-nine people. Can you imagine their last moments? What they thought when they knew they were going down?'

'If they went down.'

'Oh, you think they're still out there on a mystery flight path somewhere, a month later?'

'Sorry. I was being flippant.'

'It's not something to joke about. It's crazy. I mean, listen to this. "*Goodnight Malaysian three seven zero.*" That's the last single thing they called in. After that, nothing.'

'Is there some news?'

'The report's come out, that's all. They left it three hours and fifty-two minutes to get the search and rescue going. Can you believe that? The Australian prime minister is "*baffled and confused*". I'll say.'

He held up a radar image. There was a dot and a line, then nothing.

I took off my sunglasses and looked at the dot, then I lay back on the grass and stared at the sky.

My first ultrasound scan showed a dot just like the one on Robert's radar image. For the final scan, when my husband and

I were told Phoebe had died, there was a consultant obstetrician, and with him, two registrars. Taking it in turns, they rolled a probe over my belly and discussed what they could see. Then the machine was switched off and the registrars walked out. The screen blinked twice, then was blank. 'Viable' was the word the consultant used, turning his face away. 'Not viable.'

Because I was flat on my back in the park, my tears rolled into my ears. Robert was talking, but instead of listening, I noticed the way the hot salt water tickled the skin on the sides of my face. It pooled first in my outer ear then it ran right in, so his voice was distant.

I sat up and shook my head. Tuning in, I heard him repeat three words.

'Aviate. Navigate. Communicate. You got that?' He saw my blank face. 'Have you been listening to anything I'm saying? One more time. Aviate: make sure you are alert and oriented. Navigate: always know your geographical location. Communicate: report in – that is, tell the control tower where you are. Those are your basics, right there.'

I nodded.

'Well,' Robert said, 'I'm just trying to tell you the basics.'

I didn't say anything. Robert pointed to our left. I looked at the reading couple again. Occasionally, one of them picked up a wine glass and took a sip, or turned another page, but otherwise they were still.

'They're like two adjoining walls in the corner of a room,' Robert said. 'Look. They're actually holding each other up.' I could see what he meant: if one of them was to shift their position, the other would fall. We watched them, then Robert said, 'Children are the coving.'

'I'm sorry?'

'I've worked something out.' He'd slipped off his shoes and socks, and was sitting cross-legged. He shrugged his shoulders up, and down, then he sighed. 'Here's the thing. If a marriage is like a room in a house, then the child is like the coving. You sand the walls and paint the room. Maybe a new ceiling rose, around the light. Different drapes, to match the new colour. The very last thing you do is fix up the coving, right? Your room is perfect. Then a few years later, the kid goes to college, and you decide to redesign the interior. The coving comes down and you see the whole thing differently. The walls are uneven. They don't join properly. They're not aligned right. You couldn't see it before, but now you do. There's gaps in places there shouldn't be, and everything is – it's a mess. Listen to me, Elizabeth.' He scratched the side of his face. 'You've just turned forty, right? I remember my fortieth birthday like it was this morning. I'd worked on our house until there was nothing left to do. Philippe was happy, Lena was beautiful. I was doing well at the firm. My parents were healthy. Everyone was – We were all OK. I came downstairs that morning and I walked into the living room. Lena and Philippe were sitting there. Everything in the picture was perfect. But you know what? It was like it was someone else's life. Now the whole goddam thing is broken up. The house is gone, the walls are gone, and the picture frame is on the floor, smashed into pieces.'

On the Sunday afternoon he went to Paris. As we said goodbye I asked him to bring me a present.

'What kind of present?'

'Oh, nothing fancy. A leaf. Bring me a leaf from the Tuileries Gardens.'

'I can't!'

'Why not?'

'Who does that?'

'Don't, then.'

'A leaf? Who asks someone to bring them a leaf?'

After dinner with friends that evening, and meetings on the Monday, he would fly to Tokyo.

My flatmate was having a party I didn't feel like being at, so I did something I'd never done, and accepted Robert's offer of his place for the week he was away.

His postcard from Paris arrived Tuesday. On its face was a photograph of Giacometti's *L'objet invisible*. A doleful figure was perched on an elongated chair. The chair was cast in the same dull bronze as the figure, whose hands were held aloft and slightly apart. The caption on the reverse was its fuller title, *Mains tenant le vide*. Other than my name and address, Robert's only inscription was a square drawn in black felt tip.

That evening after the library, I spread my notes on the living-room floor. Kneeling there, I noticed the manila pages of his prenup poking from under the coffee table. The agreement, still bound with its pink ribbon, had been placed on top of a stack of hardback architecture books.

All the next day in the library, the little flash of pink was in and out of my mind. At the apartment again, I pushed the agreement further under the coffee table and looked on Robert's shelves for something to read before dinner. In a book by Adam Phillips, Robert had underlined passages. '*If you want to make someone fall for you,*' one of the passages read, '*intrude, invade, insert yourself.*'

I sat with the book in my hands for some time, thinking about the stream of empty hotel envelopes Robert had sent me from his trips. Once, he'd enclosed a room-service slip with a heart scrawled in the corner, our initials entwined inside it. Another time there was a subway ticket from New

York, and a map of Manhattan on a plastic card. On a trip to Toronto he'd sent a chocolate-bar wrapper in a tissue-paper envelope. Turning it over, I had just been able to make out the letters 'L–O–V–E' stamped into the foil, intaglio-style.

I'd always imagined those things to be proxies for the letters he hadn't had time to write. That evening in his apartment, though, I read further in the Adam Phillips. *'Take every opportunity to put yourself in their field of vision,'* the underlined extract concluded. *'Interfere with every aspect of their life.'*

I put the book away and ate dinner at the breakfast bar. I thought of his conquest of Lena. 'It didn't matter what,' he'd said, 'as long as there was something on her doormat every day, with my name on the back.'

He'd printed the photos of our picnic. Flicking through them while I ate, my polka-dot top was all I saw.

I had a bath after dinner. Drying myself, I took the towel from between my legs and a string of mucus, like egg white, flicked onto my inner thigh. Realising what day of my cycle I was on, I stretched the mucus between my fingers to two, maybe two and a half inches. I pulled on a pair of Robert's pyjamas. I wrapped myself in his kimono robe and put his orange-green fine wool scarf around my neck. Wearing his socks pulled up over my knees, I lay on the living-room sofa under Lena's silk-fur throw, and I read the prenup through.

When he'd sent for his copy of the agreement in March, he'd offered to read it out to me but I'd said no. He'd given me a summary instead, but I hadn't really listened. Now, I only half read it. Skipping whole paragraphs, I glimpsed a line that was familiar: regardless of the pair's individual finances, and without recourse to them, the assets of the marriage would be split precisely in two.

I had discovered nothing new by looking at it, but it felt strange to have read it in his absence. I pulled Lena's throw up and over my face. It was heavy, and as my temperature rose, I remembered Robert telling me how, on his wedding day, he'd brushed off his mother's warning about the precariousness of his new-found wealth, and I thought of Robert signing it.

Lying there on his sofa, I remembered Robert coming back from Washington in February. He'd shown me photographs of Philippe, and I'd been struck by how proud he was of his son's height. The subject had come up more than once. 'It's all because of Lena,' Robert had said. 'I mean, the guy's three inches taller than me! It's amazing.'

'Boys always grow taller than their mothers,' I'd said.

Robert had shown me those photographs a few times, always with the exact same commentary: Philippe had his mother to thank for his height, but it was Robert who had given him his thick, black hair and his dark brown eyes. 'He must have girls going crazy for those eyes!' he'd laughed. 'I know I did when I was his age! I'm telling you, look at 'em. But I never had quite his height. That would've been something.'

Now, with my own eyes shut tight and my temperature still rising, I pictured his beautiful, tall American boy, and I imagined his beginning, and the fusing of those genes that had made him what he was. I pictured the tiny new life, half-Lena, half-Robert, burrowing its way into the lining of her womb. I saw it take its first taste of her hot red blood, then I realised: whatever else Robert was entitled to under the prenup, he was quite within his rights to claim his half of Philippe.

My breathing grew shallow. I imagined myself as a surgeon holding a scalpel to Philippe's face. Pressing hard at a point just beneath the young man's hairline, until both layers of skin were pierced, I would dig and drag, tracking a line down the front of his body. Then I would work the scalpel in the other direction, digging a line up and over the top of his head and all the way down his back.

Returning to the site of my first incision, I would reach my fingers under the flaps of skin and peel away the whole of it, in much the same way as one might skin a mango: lifting and ripping, then reaching my fingers in further, and lifting and ripping again.

Next, I would raise a hatchet above the newly bare skull and bring it down sharply. Provided I was fast enough, and my aim sufficiently exact, Philippe's skull would fall into equal parts, clean as a watermelon chopped in two.

The final severing (of the whole of the body from the neck down) would require a tool not unlike Robert's angle grinder, and a stand of the sort found in a bicycle-repair workshop, so that Philippe might be held firmly in place.

Because there would be sparks from the grinder, I would be masked. As well as my surgical gloves, I would wear a rubber apron. The prenup required a precise separation, so I'd have to take my time: holding the grinder against myself, to better sense its weight and motion, I would saw from the top down steadily, ignoring the spray of flesh and bone.

When my ex-husband and I bought our flat, we were asked a question by our conveyancing solicitor that we later laughed about. Did we want to own our home jointly, so that we each had an equal right to the whole asset, or would we prefer to own it in different quantifiable portions, so that our shares might one day be divided?

Choosing the first option without thinking, we were as careless in our happiness as Robert had been, signing his prenup without so much as reading it.

In our final week together, my husband and I trailed around the flat, pointing.

'You can have that, if I can have this.'

A pair of wedding-gift wine glasses, etched as finely as spiders' webs, were touched together one last time to hear the particular ring they made, then just as easily wrapped separately. A couple of pottery teacups, one light blue one dark, took us two seconds to divide.

We used Post-it notes to record our decisions about furniture. The flat took on a festive appearance, as though we were putting up bunting for a party. When the notes dwindled, I found a bag of Christmas wrapping paper with balls of ribbon. He took the dark green spool, and I the red. Dusk fell outside as we worked, tying bows around what remained: the stem of a standard lamp; an armchair; a globe he had found in Stanford's when we'd first moved to London a decade ago.

'So we know where we are,' he'd said when he'd brought it home. 'It is absolutely essential that we know where we are at all times,' then he'd laughed, and made me laugh.

The division of our books was more difficult. Contemplating the wall of volumes, laid down over the years like heavy layers of granite, we were made too unhappy by the idea of their division and decided to wait until the flat was sold.

At certain times of day, the dusky white-green of our bedroom walls matched the insides of the broad beans in our garden, which we'd harvested and shelled together. Standing in the room on what would be my final visit, after I'd collected together my house plants, and a picture I'd left on the wall, I closed the curtains. I waited until the sun had flooded through the fabric and filled the whole of the room.

The colour of the walls was thrown around, and the space was made gold-white, as though I was hidden inside one of those little pods.

Later, having left the flat and locked the front door, I saw my husband standing on the pavement.

We had agreed by email that I would drop the keys through the letter box. I'd lingered in the bedroom, though, in that white-green haze, and he'd arrived home earlier than planned.

We stood and stared.

Then we walked towards one another and he moved to kiss me but I turned my head slightly and his kiss fell on my cheek.

Two years on, he found a job abroad and sold the flat. We took our library to pieces, and his new girlfriend helped him to pack. When he phoned me from the ferry terminal, I could hear that he was crying, but there was a bird, or a seagull, and I couldn't make out what he was saying.

The morning after that phone call, I experienced a loss of sensation down the whole of my right-hand side. Next came a burning pain over the same area, which lasted six weeks. Once or twice that summer, small soft clumps of my hair fell out.

'Without Philippe,' Robert had said to me once, 'I'm Calvino's Invisible Knight.' I hadn't understood at the time, but that evening in Robert's apartment, holding the prenup in my hands, I saw the whole thing clearly: because he couldn't risk losing this boy, without whom he would be nothing, a child with a new partner simply wasn't an option. If Robert's relationship with Philippe was to be protected, the self he must present was the self he had always been: a father to his only son, and never to any other.

At dinner the night he got back from Tokyo, he said he'd missed me, and what about a few days away together?

'Let's go to Nice,' I said. 'We could have a dip. Lie in the sun for a day and come back tanned.'

'Could we try Cornwall?'

'Cornwall? In May? The sea will be like ice. There's always Spain.'

'Well,' he said. 'Here's the thing.'

He'd been invited to friends at Bodinnick, on the south-east Cornish coast, and wanted to take me with him.

'Who are they?'

'Oh, some writers, a few artists.'

'How many?'

'A houseful. Some of them I'll know, some of them I won't. I'll check exactly who, if you want. The hosts are friends of ours.'

'"Ours"?'

'Friends of Lena's.'

'Friends of yours, or friends of Lena's?'

'Both.'

'Will she be there?'

'Of course not!'

'They invited me?'

'Not exactly.'

'What, then?'

'I asked if I could bring you, and they said yes.'

We left it until the following evening, when he said he ought to reply.

'How long?' I asked.

'Three nights.'

'Can I just come for two?'

'Why?'

'I haven't planned to take time off this month. I need to hand in a draft.'

'Not really.'

'Not really what?'

'You can't really come for two nights. Either come for three, or don't come.'

'What?'

'It's just how it is. It's a whole weekend, planned. You know, meals, walks. Transport.'

'It's just a weekend with friends, right? Why can't I just head back the day before you?'

'It's a really special place. I'd love you to see it properly.' I didn't answer. 'If you can't come, that's just fine. You can meet them another time.'

'Really?'

'Really.'

'How much will you mind if I turn you down?'

'Hmmmmm.' He smiled, and began to raise his hand from the tabletop. When it reached his shoulder, he continued. I leaned in and started to kiss him, and he brought it back down. 'You do what you gotta do, honey.'

'If I come, can I bring work?'

'You can. Not a whole lot, though.'

'I'll come. I'll spend one day of the three working, OK?'

'We don't need to travel first class,' I said when he told me about the tickets. 'They must've cost –'

'There's a pickup when we get there. Everyone's travelling on the same train. It's five hours, honey. It would be weird if we were the only ones not in first.'

'How do you know everyone else will?'
'Trust me.'

At Paddington, I found him by the information desk. I walked towards him but he looked over my head, searching the crowd. I went a few steps closer, but still I was invisible. He jumped when I touched his arm.

'How do you do that?'

'Do what?'

'Creep up on me like that.' Then he held me, and kissed me.

A woman walked into our carriage who knew Robert. He kissed her on both cheeks. Lifting her bag, he started to put it in the overhead rack but she stopped him.

'Really!' he said, lifting it back up. 'Let me help you!'

'No, thank you. It's fine. I just need –'

There was a tug of war, until he realised she wanted something out of it. He let her, then he tried again but she said, 'Actually, thanks ever so.' She smiled. 'I'll just put it under my seat.'

'OK!' he said. 'Well, if you need a hand, you know where to find me!'

Sitting down again, he told me she was a magazine editor. 'She's probably used to doing her own thing.'

I read my manuscript, making pencil marks of what I needed to fix that weekend. He read a novel by our middle-aged male host-to-be, about a middle-aged male novelist's midlife crisis.

On the pickup in Cornwall, which was a small minibus with velvet seats, our driver wore a tweed suit, and spoke into a wire that ran from an earpiece. The magazine editor sat next to me. She said just enough for me to understand she was a friend of Lena's, rather than Robert's. She wasn't unkind, but she did seem puzzled at my being there.

I looked around. Robert was in the back row. He was deep in conversation with a dark-haired woman of about his age, who seemed to be on her own. I looked some more until he caught my eye. He half raised a hand, then he continued his conversation.

There was a mist, and I saw nothing of the landscape. When we reached our destination, the sky was pitch, without a single star, so it wasn't until the morning that I would have any idea of where we were.

At dinner there was a seating plan.

Our host's wife, Lucy, took the head of the table; our host, Peter, the other end. Neither of us were anywhere near either of them. Later, in bed, Robert reported that he'd found himself next to the wife of an old acquaintance of his. It was the old acquaintance's second marriage, and his new wife was in her early forties. Instead of having their own children, which is what she'd wanted, she had settled to be stepmother to his. When Robert had pushed her on her readiness to compromise, she'd explained that his acquaintance had offered her a different kind of happiness.

In London, they lived in Holland Park in a house that was known for its art, and where they sometimes gave private fundraisers. In Paris there was a flat in Neuilly-sur-Seine. When they travelled elsewhere, properties were made available by his friends as he, or she, desired.

'He gives her experiences she'd never have had without him,' Robert said. 'She seemed very happy. By the way, did you think about my next trip to Washington?' He rolled over the bed to where I was, and put his hand between my legs. 'Will you come? It would be so much fun.'

At sunrise, while Robert slept on, I slipped behind the curtains. The house was positioned at the head of a wide creek, which was dry at that hour. The creek's bed had been ribbed by the departing tide. In the far distance, it met a bend and disappeared. Woods rose steeply on either side, and I could see some movement in the trees: a fox showed itself; further in and larger, something else made a crashing noise. I pulled on my clothes and went out.

A heron stood in the mud. I watched it, then I walked along the bank until the woods became too thick, and the path petered out. Turning, I saw that the house, which was set above the creek, was much larger than I'd realised. Emerging from behind the western wing was a low yew hedge and what looked to be the start of a formal garden. The building was in soft stone, the colour of chalk. A boathouse was built into its lower parts, so that when the tide was in, entry could be gained directly from the water.

There was the sound of beating wings, then there was silence.

I scanned the banks but could see no other dwellings. Taking the path the other way, I walked beyond the creek's mouth and into the woods, then the trees closed in and I was afraid I would be lost.

At the house again, our bedroom was empty. Robert had left a note.

Did you forget Peter said 9am? If we'd gone to breakfast at the same time, we could've sat together.

I threw the note away, then I showered and went downstairs.

Peter and Lucy had swapped places. From the head of the table, Peter watched me take the last of the strawberries. He signalled to a uniformed attendant, who disappeared and reappeared with a plate piled with berries the size of billiard balls.

Robert was on the other side of the table from me, in between a much older man and the dark-haired woman he'd sat with on the minibus. A few of the guests were reading newspapers, but Robert's little group were talking. I didn't follow everything that was said, but I could just make out the woman's Italian accent. Listening more clearly, I heard her say something about her husband, an artist, who had stayed behind in Siena. She often did trips on her own, she told Robert. While she spoke she brushed Robert's arm from time to time, or laid her hand on his.

Once, he looked at me and said, 'What do you think, honey?' but I had drifted off, and had no idea what he was asking about. 'Don't be shy now,' he said, cracking a smile. 'Do you agree with Maddalena, or with me?'

'You, Robert,' Maddalena said, tilting her chin. 'Of course she agrees with you.'

'Well?' Robert said. 'Come on, honey. Which is it to be?'

To my relief, Peter stood up at exactly that moment and tapped his glass with a spoon. At half past ten, he announced, Lucy would be happy to show the walled garden to anyone who was interested, and some of the grounds beyond. Lunch would be served at 1 p.m., when we were to take the same seats as we had for the previous night's dinner, but for the fact the men should move two places to their left. At half past two, Peter himself would lead a walk through the estate's woods as far as Lantic Bay.

The table was cleared. Robert stood to pull back Maddalena's chair. She said something in a low voice, and he laughed.

On the stairs, going to get our walking things, Robert put his hand on my head. 'You can't work this morning. You're not –'

'Obviously,' I said. 'I want to see the garden. I want to see the sea. I'd rather do it without Peter's stopwatch, but hey. I'll work on the last day. Should I let him know now, so he can schedule it?'

Long since fallen into disuse, the garden was a remnant from a neighbouring estate. It had required complete restoration when Peter and Lucy bought the property.

Now, the vegetable beds were stacked with irises and peonies. On our arrival, I'd noticed straight away that every surface of every room was stuffed with them cut into vases. Seeing the scale on which they were grown made the whole thing seem more reasonable.

We took in the rest of the house's immediate grounds. Strolling back to lunch, Robert talked only to Maddalena. I drew near and heard him say, 'Aviate. Navigate. Communicate!'

'*Davvero?*' Her hand was on his arm again. '*È così semplice?*'

'Yes, it really is that simple! Well, almost. It's like this. Number one. Aviate.'

Knowing the rest, I let them go on ahead.

On the walk to Lantic Bay, I attached myself to one then another of the small groups that formed. The conversation in each was the same: the upkeep and management of the guests' own estates in France, Italy and Germany. Woods in particular featured heavily, and the replacing of avenues of trees blighted by one disease or another. A couple from Paris were concerned about re-landscaping their property in Avignon; if the appearance of their own boating lake was to be maintained, a series of ponds would have to be drained and moved. The view from the riverbank would be altered beyond what had been deemed reasonable by the district's conservation lobby, and local resistance was unexpectedly fierce. Robert listened, then made some suggestions and said he'd be happy to look over the plans.

The lake-owners asked him where in London he had bought property, since his split from Lena. 'Oh, well,' he said. 'I'm biding my time. I don't know where Philippe will be next year. So there's no hurry.'

I tried to take his hand then, but he brushed me away so I hung back for the next group.

Ahead of our return from the walk, a candle from a Parisian perfume house had been lit in our room. There was another in our bathroom, giving off the same scent. While Robert read further in Peter's novel, which he'd begun on the train, I drew a bath. I sat on the side to see it fill, and added a few drops of oil from a glass bottle that was there. After a minute in the oil-perfumed steam, which was the same as the candles but only heavier, I could barely breathe. When Robert heard me trying to open the window, he came in.

'Here, let me help you.' He struggled, then he said, 'Do you really need it open?'

'I blew the candle out but the oil's the same.'

'You don't like it?'

'It's too much. I feel sick. By the way, did you just tut, before you asked me that? Did you actually tut?' I tried the window again myself, pushing harder. He put his hands to his head. 'It's OK, Robert. It's just a window.'

'It's a fifteenth-century window, actually.'

'Jesus. Will you give me a break? I've done it.' The air rushed in. 'It's fine. It will apparently live to see another century.'

In bed that night, Robert was full of talk of Peter, whom he'd sat with in the library after dinner. The two of them had been so huddled away on a corner sofa, and so deep in conversation, I'd gone upstairs to make notes on my manuscript. He came in and, seeing that I was working, picked up Peter's novel again. He broke off once, to ask me if I thought writing was an antisocial pursuit. Didn't it, he asked, take the writer away from the world? Wasn't it, therefore, the most selfish of occupations? 'I'm not saying Peter's like that,' he interrupted himself. 'He could talk all night. If you asked him to, he would. But all this time he spent, writing this, you know?'

'Uh-huh,' I said, half hearing him.

'It's a withdrawal from the world. Both of you. You're shutting yourself –'

'Honey, can I just get this done? Then I'm all yours.'

He read some more. Later, while I undressed, he finished Peter's book. Then he turned out the light and asked me to walk away from him and hide somewhere.

'What?'

'I want to come find you.'

'Hide-and-seek?'

'Sex hide-and-seek. It'd be fun.'

'It'd be weird.'

'Why? Come on, honey. We're in this amazing room. We could –'

'Is it in Peter's book? Is that what made you think of it?'

'Not exactly.'

'What do you mean, not exactly?'

'He writes about sex. Not like that, though.'

'How, then?'

He switched on his bedside lamp, and reached for the book. 'You know what? It's one of the things he gets completely right. Non-procreational sex.'

'I'm sorry?'

'When you've already had a kid, and you know you're never going to have another one, sex is just different. You wouldn't understand. It's a guy thing. I know exactly what he means. The way he describes it is how it is for me, with you. It's recreational.'

Before that moment, I had been winded only once in my life. Approaching the close of play in the last match in a school tournament, I'd twisted and jumped at the same time as my marker. Her fists, aiming to punch the netball from my hands, had risen up and made contact with my stomach, just below my ribcage.

On the ground afterwards, trying to get some breath, the intensity of the pain made my eyes run, as though someone had switched on a tap.

'I'm not crying,' I said, when everyone leaned over me. 'It's my eyes, you know. I'm not crying.'

That night at Bodinnick, I didn't say a word. The window was still open from my bath and there was the sound of the creek, going out with the tide.

It was only when he sat up in the bed, flicking through Peter's book for a passage he wanted to reread, that I realised he had no idea what he'd done by his inadvertent revelation.

He found the passage he was looking for, and sighed. I noticed, for the first time, how his nipples sagged slightly. 'Can I read you this, honey?'

I let him read. When he'd finished, I said what I thought he'd like me to say. He told me he agreed with me completely, and that I could borrow Peter's novel right away. I said I'd love to; I had been looking for something new to read for a while.

'Perfect timing,' he said then, turning off the lamp. I heard him move towards me. 'So what about it? You wanna play hide-and-seek?'

There was the sound of the creek again, from the window.

'Actually, honey,' I said quietly, 'we walked a long way today. Is it OK if we just crash out?'

'If that's what you want. Do you mind if I read some more? I'll keep the light low.'

'Read as long as you like. I could sleep through thunder and lightning tonight. It's the sea air, I think. Sea air always does this to me.'

The bed was wide enough for me to lie apart from him. In the morning, there was a note beside my pillow.

I've gone for a run with Peter. Don't wait for me, honey, if you get hungry, OK? See you at breakfast.

The following day, I was loaned a small office. The only pieces of furniture were a chair and an old oak desk, covered in green leather. On its surface were a telephone, a glass lamp, and a single sheet of paper with a typed list of phone numbers.

Woods … Gardener … Maintenance … Games … Pont Creek Cottage … Dugard & Sons (meat).

All morning, Peter used the room as a cut-through to another part of the house. At first, he seemed bemused, and apologised, saying he had forgotten I was in there. The next time, he expressed his amazement that I was still working. By his fifth visit, his tone had become disdainful.

'Not sure why you came, really, if you've so much on your plate.'

That afternoon, he took everyone else on another walk to Lantic Bay. Having been distracted by Peter's visits, I was pleased to catch up, and was surprised by the bell for cocktails.

Robert was pacing our room.

He looked at me, then looked at his watch. Without saying a word, he went downstairs.

I followed not long after. In the drawing room everyone was gathered in a ring, laughing. Looking over someone's shoulder, I saw Maddalena. Robert was holding her hand.

'One more time,' Peter called out, glancing at me.

'Like this?' Robert said, bowing his head to Maddalena's hand and kissing it lightly.

'*Sei davvero bravo.*' She laughed, a low laugh, like little bells.

Everyone clapped and drifted away: to the window, admiring the gardens, or to the drinks cabinet, to make another cocktail. Robert and Maddalena went to the sofa. When I sat with them, Robert turned his back.

I stayed where I was, deliberately not taking the hint.

Robert leaned in and admired Maddalena's necklace.

As I'd dressed for dinner, I'd noticed a small moth hole in my dress; it had been too late to change, and in any case, I'd brought nothing else. Now, on the sofa, I pressed my finger into the hole and made it larger. Gazing at my flat black shoes, which were slightly scuffed, I interrupted.

'Maddalena, may I ask you a question? Is your estate in Tuscany, or Umbria?'

She looked at me, but instead of answering my question, turned more towards Robert and said to him, 'You must come again. Your son was so small when you visited the last time, with Lena.' Then she looked at me again. 'And you,' she said sweetly. She took a short, sharp breath, and took my hand. 'Please say you will.'

At lunch on the last day, Peter announced that a farewell 'Nursery Tea' would be held before we were driven back to the station for the night train. Robert saw my face change, and leaned in to whisper, 'Put your walking boots on. I've had a different idea.'

'Won't we be in trouble?' I whispered back.

He took my hand and led me from the room, smiling and nodding at Peter. On the stairs to our room he said, 'I don't care if we're in trouble. You've tagged along and come all this way. You've done so well with everyone. I want to make it up to you.'

Tiptoeing back down, we made sure the hall was clear then we walked quietly from the house. We headed off through the woods for an hour or more, then looped back round and down to the creek. At the very end of the path, where the creek met the sea, there was a small strip of sand. The sun was on it, and we took off our boots and socks. He held my hand, and we ran to the end of the strip. Robert took a stick and drew shapes on the sand, explaining how the action of the departing tide caused the particular patterns that were there. Then he stopped explaining and used the stick to carve a heart instead, with our initials at the centre.

When he was done, we found a rock to sit on while we put on our boots. Robert stroked the sand from my feet.

Lacing up my boots again, I told him about having done the same in Tavira, with my neighbour's daughter, then I joked that people would pay good money for such a service, on English beaches up and down the country. He could paint a sign, I said. He'd make millions.

'I'm not kidding! Spend a summer as a foot-stroker, and you'd be able to buy yourself a place in London, no problem. If you ever come back, that's what you should do! You'd cover your first-class train fare, at least.'

'Imagine, though,' he said, laughing at my joke, 'if we did come back, in a year, say. Imagine if the exact same group of people came here again. How would we all have changed? What would everyone be doing?'

That was when, without meaning to, I found myself sketching him a scene, just for a moment, of us returning with our child, not quite a year old, and introducing it to his friends.

'It would be so much fun,' I said, leaning in to him and taking his hand, 'to come back with a baby. It would sleep all the way on the train, and you could carry it on your back and we could take it on Peter's walk to Lantic Bay.'

I talked some more, about there being enough room in our enormous bed for it to sleep with us, and how the bath was so large, I could bathe with it. When I asked him for a name, or a few to choose between, and which would he most want, a boy or a girl, he held me tighter and, saying nothing at all, kissed the top of my head.

We stayed that way for some time, then Robert stood.

'Come on, honey.' He pulled me up. 'Missing the Nursery Tea was one thing, but if we're late for our ride, we really *will* be in trouble. Race you. Loser does the winner's packing,' and he was gone. Watching him jog across the sand, I knew for certain that he'd already reached his decision about our deal, quite some time ago, and that he'd been perfectly aware that my sketching the scenes I'd sketched for him, sitting on the rock, had been my way of telling him I knew.

On the return drive to Penzance, I sat up front with the driver, who spoke softly into his mouthpiece all the way.

Robert sat at the back, in between the magazine editor and Maddalena. From time to time I heard Maddalena's soft, low laugh.

We were in town the following Saturday. My translator friends from Lisbon were over for a book launch: some short stories about football, taken from the Portuguese. When the invitation had come, I'd asked Robert right away and he'd accepted. That Saturday, for the first time ever in our relationship, he told me he'd accidentally double-booked, and there was nothing to be done. Instead of my friend's book launch, then, he went to a soiree at the opera director's apartment in Clerkenwell with his friend Juliet. He called partway through the evening, but I missed him. When I called back there was no answer.

On the Sunday, we were to meet at Oxford Circus, to walk to a Marylebone restaurant for Juliet's birthday lunch. The invitation had said, 'jacket and tie, ladies – formal', but it was the first hot day of the year, and I wore a sundress and sandals.

Juliet's a great timekeeper, his text had said. *Don't be tardy.* He was standing in the shade when I arrived, almost diagonally opposite where we first kissed in December. Pulling at his tie, he saw what I was wearing and frowned. When I walked towards him he looked away.

Just round the corner, he found a bench and asked me to sit with him. There, in the full sun, twenty-five minutes before the lunch was due to begin, he said it.

'I can't have a child with you. I can't do that again. I promised I'd tell you if I decided, and I'm telling you now.'

At the soiree the previous evening, he explained, there had been a couple with their newborn son.

'They just brought him for a half-hour. To say hello, and introduce him. They were so – They were so wrapped up in him. In each other. I can't do that again. I did it once already. They were right to be like that. It's how they should have been. It's how you have to be, when you have – I can't do it over. I want to spend the rest of my life looking out at the world, not in. I want to connect, not close myself away.'

I'd started to cry as soon as he'd begun. Now, frustrated at myself, I tried to stop but couldn't. 'But you drew the floor plan.'

'I what, honey?' He had his hand on my thigh.

'Of our apartment, where we would live. You drew the plan for our apartment. With the long corridor and the carpet in my room.'

'I was only painting pictures, honey. That's what you asked me to do.'

'I thought you wanted to. I thought you wanted us – I thought that's why you did it.'

'I did it so I could see what it looked like. I thought I might have liked how it looked.'

Then I cried properly, and it was some time before I stopped. When he tugged my elbow, I saw that he was looking at his watch.

'Come on, honey. I told you Juliet's a timekeeper.'

'What?'

'We can't be late.'

My eyes were hurting, and my vision blurred. 'Are you serious?'

'Come on. If we walk fast, we'll get there for the pre-lunch drinks.'

'You really think I'd come? Now, after this?'

'You have to! Juliet will have gone to a lot of trouble for this. It's a small group. It's a smart place.'

'I'm going home, Robert. I'm leaving.'

And that was when I finally did what Juliet had said I should, at the opera director's party: I made up my mind, and walked away.

I took a slow route, through Regent's Park. Then I went to Magali's and Olivier's club for the evening. Afterwards, I stayed over at their place. In the morning when Robert Skyped, I was hung-over.

'I'm in free fall,' I said. 'I feel like –' I was crying too much to speak clearly. 'I feel – There was a gale last night, in my head. It was so loud and everything fell.'

'I'm sorry,' he said. He was leaning in to the screen, to inspect my face in the same way as he'd inspected my body once, like an artist or a student of anatomy. He turned his head slightly to one side, inspecting me from a different angle, like a raptor. He pulled his hands through his hair.

'You're so beautiful, and I'm so sorry.'

Epilogue

<u>*If you are in a bad storm at sea*</u>

Note your present compass course. With your face to the wind, extend your right arm outwards from the side of your body, until it is parallel to the deck. If you are in the northern hemisphere, you are now pointing towards the low-pressure centre of the storm. 2. Keeping the same compass course, repeat the observation every half-hour, and note any changes in the direction of the wind. If the wind is veering (turning towards the right), then steer a course keeping your starboard flank towards the wind. If the wind is backing (turning towards the left), then steer a course with your starboard bow towards the wind. 3. These actions will take you towards the safe quadrant of the storm, where winds, waves, and tidal surges will be easier.

Frank Johnson, *Sailing by Hand,*
A Beginner's Manual

It had ended so simply. In the days that followed, I woke with the sun and couldn't sleep again.

There were meetings when we embraced and said we loved each other but couldn't be together. Some days, things seemed remarkably easy. One lunchtime in Lincoln's Inn Fields, he said he'd been thinking about the idea of us living together.

'Are you crazy?'

'It struck me there were two choices. We could have tried "friends with benefits", or we could have moved in. So then I thought about the moving-in option, and it occurred to me it might be exactly what we need. Like lancing a boil.'

'We've broken up.'

'We have?'

'You know we have. But let's be friends. Real friends, I mean, not in the way people say they will, then aren't. Life's so short. Why shouldn't we try? What else matters?'

He said he didn't know if he could do that, and he asked me what exactly it would mean. I said we could have dinners and movies in the way that friends did, but more than that: we could look out for one another, and watch each other's backs.

We emailed through the early summer, keeping up with the small details of our lives, passing on what he called items of note, but which were mainly anecdotes.

In my memory of that time, May and June blur together. Things we'd arranged had to be cancelled, and flights let go. There were invitations we'd accepted as a couple, so that one of us would pull out each time.

At a long midsummer picnic, we lay and held each other, and talked of trying again. He suggested ideas for where we might live, and how we could arrange our lives. Then I rested my head on his shoulder and his chest. His breath was warm on the bridge of my nose, and it lulled me to sleep.

When we woke, we said all our problems were workable. We walked to the Underground station hand in hand. On the Tube, though, we agreed we'd only hurt each other. We got to my stop and I stood to go but he held my arm.

'Please. Will you come stay the night?'

I was confused and wanted to say yes. Instead, in the second before the doors closed, I stepped from the carriage then I turned to look at him. 'Don't forget me.'

Weeks passed, and I wrote to ask after his preparation for the trip with Philippe, and to tell him I was still finding things difficult.

'*To say it "hurts like hell",*' I closed, '*goes nowhere to describe this feeling.*'

He wrote back:

Honey, I'm so sorry you're hurting. Me too. It will get better, I hope, for both of us, when everything isn't so raw.

Thank you for asking about my trip. I am looking forward to it, but am also anxious as I notice from my research that the slack-tides aren't scheduled to happen during broad daylight, when I was hoping to transit Woods Hole. I may have to wait out the strong floods and ebbs by standing safely off the ledges until just after dawn or before dusk.

R

Yes, it will get better. But I had let myself think I would stand off the ledges with you somewhere until just before dusk. That you'd bring us in to safe harbour and rock us to sleep. That there would be the sound of a rope straining, or of other boats yawling.

I think of your shoulders, and your chest, and how they felt under my hands. And I think of your breath in sleep, and what it was to be found when you turned and reached for me.

    E

Dear honey, what do we do? I miss you, but I also want to protect myself, and keep myself from hurting you any more than I do now.

    R

R,
I guess we do nothing. That's what we do.

    E

The last time I saw him it was raining.

I'd been leaving a book launch in Pall Mall and had accidentally phoned his number. In the process of asking the doorman if he had a spare umbrella, and which was closer, Green Park or Piccadilly, I'd leaned against the counter with my bag in front of me. My phone, which was in my bag, dialled his number.

Walking to Piccadilly, I picked up his message saying that I had called him ten separate times. Each time he'd answered, he'd heard muffled voices giving what sounded like directions, or instructions. By the fifth time, he'd begun to imagine I was being kidnapped and was making attempts to send him a signal. I phoned him back straight away.

'I'm sorry!' I laughed, and tried to explain. 'I'm so sorry!'

'You wanna celebrate your freedom? Let's get dinner!'

'Yes, OK. Well, I'm done here, and I guess technically I'm free. So, OK, why not?'

He met me from the Tube with his umbrella, and walked with his arm around me. It was late, and at the restaurant near his apartment, where we'd eaten once before, we were the only customers.

I said it was nice to meet up, and it had been good of him to check I wasn't actually being kidnapped.

But when we'd ordered, I said it was hard to see him, and it would be best if we didn't meet again for a long time.

'How long?'

'Maybe six months? A year? I don't know.'

'There were so many things we could have done for each other.'

'There were, I know.'

'There are, honey. I mean there still are.'

I shook my head. He carried on, and said it would be too fast an ending. That my proposal we shouldn't meet for a year was too draconian.

'It was already a shock, honey. We were there, then we were at zero, you know? If we can't see each other for that long –'

'What do you mean? What do you want?'

'I want you.'

'Give me a break. We can't talk if you're –'

'OK, here's what I mean. If I see you, I want you. So you have to set the speed. You're more vulnerable than me. It's like two runners, one fast, one slow. You're the slow one, so you choose the pace. I don't know how you feel about this. I mean, you tell me what you feel, but when you say it, I'm listening to you on a radio. You only know what it's like to be murdered if you've been murdered, you know what I'm saying?'

I couldn't understand. 'Can we talk about something else?'

'OK. Like what?'

'Like anything. Ask me a question. I miss your questions.'

'How are you sleeping?'

'OK, I guess.'

'How do you *get* to sleep?'

'Oh, you know, like I did before you came along. Music. Something – Anything really. Anything quiet. And you? Have you gone back to *Dexter*?'

'Absolutely not!' He looked over his shoulder. 'Talking of sleep, we should let these people close up. I'm sure they have homes to go to.' Then he stared at me. 'Will you come back to my place? Just to talk?'

I glanced around the room. The tables had been cleared and the chairs stacked. The waiter was standing at the till.

I looked at Robert, then I said, 'No, thank you. I won't.'

'You're just gonna say goodnight? Just like that, here?'

'Just like that.' I laughed a little. 'Don't be sad. I have to – Unless you want to walk me to the Tube.'

He took me to the corner of the street. There, I said he should take the turning for his apartment after all, and I'd be fine; the rain had held off, there was no need. Before he could try to change my mind, I'd reached up and kissed him, then I was running across the road as the lights changed and I'd slipped into a group of people and was gone.

Walking home at the other end, I was caught in a downpour. I was ill for a week, and the whole thing with Robert felt worse, not better. Then there was a phone call, which eased things.

He talked about *Chapman's* at first, and joked that he was reading it metaphorically now.

'Every one of those goddam seafaring rules! I feel like I'm going crazy. It's all your fault. There was one on tides yesterday, "*The most dramatic tides are the ones where the tides from opposite bays collide in the middle.*" Oh boy. I'm just trying to nail this trip but I keep hearing your voice.'

Then he told me he'd finished *Train Dreams*, for the second time. He felt that he was at a point in his own life that was not so dissimilar to Grainier's.

'How so?' I asked.

'If I die tomorrow, someone would have to find me in my cabin. I'd lie there for weeks in the snow. But that's OK, you know.'

'No it's not. How can you say that?'

'It is, though. I've done what I was here for. I've passed on my DNA. I've made myself again, and I've learned some things too, getting older.'

I was crying, but silently. 'Like what, Robert? Tell me what you've learned.'

'No sudden movements.' He cracked a laugh and I could see his smile as he said it. I imagined him lying back on his bed, with his and Lena's dog-marked soft cotton throw, and the afternoon light through the slatted blinds. 'And paper, for recycling.'

'What about it?' I laughed a little too, then straight away I cried again.

'If you fold it before you throw it, you can get more in the bag. Don't screw up your paper.'

'I won't.'

'You promise?'

'I promise.'

'You know, honey, I really needed you. I needed to roll in your human scent to be able to be human again.'

'It still hurts, Robert.'

'It'll stop,' he said.

'How?'

'It will just happen. One day, you'll suddenly be aware of the absence of a feeling. You'll realise you haven't thought of it for months.'

'That's it?'

'That's it, honey. And you know what else? I read a thing the other day which might interest you.'

'Tell me.'

'It was an article in the *New York Times*. Says you only need three things for happiness. Wanna hear 'em?'

'Shoot.'

'One, you need something to do. Two, you need someone to love. And three, you need something to look forward to.'

I only half heard what he was telling me then: that Woods Hole was the thing he was looking forward to most; that there might be some trouble with the insurers, who weren't keen on his final destination, on account of the currents which might or might not pull them onto the rocks. Then the line was bad, suddenly, and I couldn't hear him at all. I walked around my flat, looking for a signal. There was usually one in the corner of the attic bedroom, even if it was down everywhere else. Standing on my bed, I stared through the skylight at the lights from Shoreditch, then I stared at my phone, and switched it off.

In the morning, I thought of trying again. When I switched it on there were two messages: one from Magali seeing if I wanted company that night, and if so, they could do with my help at the bar, and by the way, did I know how to make cosmopolitans? The second was from Susie: would I like a weekend away at the end of the month, just her and me? Ben was taking Tom camping, so she had some time on her hands. And if I was free that afternoon, Tom had asked if he could learn to fly a kite. Did I know, because she had absolutely no idea.

I sat at my table and watched the Bethnal Green Road wake up. The boy at the fruit stall was unloading a van. First, there were boxes of pomegranates, then big yellow pomelos and watermelons. The boy looked up. When he waved, I waved back.

That's what I'll do, I decided. I will put on my clothes, then I will go out to get a newspaper. On the way back, I will buy myself a pomegranate. I will take out the seeds, and eat them slowly. Then I will phone Susie to ask where we'll meet, and I'll go to the library for a book on how to fly a kite.

In the evening, I will find a recipe for cosmopolitans, then I will take a long bath and wash my hair. I will choose a dress to wear to the club, and I will call Magali, to say I'm on my way.

I will pick myself up, and I will begin again.

Acknowledgements

I am grateful to the Society of Authors Authors' Foundation for their generous grant in the summer of 2017, which allowed me to finish this book. Thank you to my mother, Pamela, for giving me the gift which meant I could start it. My heartfelt thanks to Anna Webber and Seren Adams for working with me on the whole of it, from its conception. Thank you, too, to Sarah Addenbrooke, Paul Anderson, Melaina Barnes, Dee Byrne, Beth Coates, James Dingle, Andrew Dobbin, Florence Dollé, Ana Fletcher, Katherine Fry, Maddy Hartley, Sara Hemming, Paula Johnson, Darian Leader, Nicola Luckhurst, Rachael McGill, Vanessa Milton, Victoria Murray-Browne, Caroline Pelletier, Charles Peyton, Rebecca Peyton, Joe Pickering, Magali Ponroy, Tim Pozzi, Adrian Smith, Nicola Solomon, Jethro Soutar, Mark Vanhoenacker, Daisy Watt, and Robert Worley. I'm very grateful to Julia Connolly for having made the book so beautiful.

penguin.co.uk/vintage